THE L

THE LION'S GATE

by

V. J. Banis

Writing as "Jan Alexander"

The Borgo Press
An Imprint of Wildside Press

MMVII

SECOND EDITION

Chapter 1

Where was Allison? Behind the grim, forbidding gate of the lions? Or had she simply disappeared in a puff of smoke?

"Mercury is in perigee," She had said, and then she had vanished without a word, without a clue, without a warning.

Peggy Conners stared at the great iron lions crouched on either side of the gates ahead of her. They were fierce, angry-looking, and they seemed a warning of violence and tragedy to anyone who dared pass beyond them.

Peggy reached out and put a hand on the wrought iron of one of the twin gates. It swung inward at her touch. For a moment, she hesitated. Then she passed through, casting an apprehensive glance upward at the lions.

Beware, we stand at the gates of hell, was the inscription above the gates.

A sudden sound in the shrubbery to her right made her start. She turned and to her amazement, there was Allison, the leaves of a tree casting shadows across her pale face—but it was Allison, unmistakably Allison.

"Allison, thank God I've found you," Peggy said. *"What on earth happened to you? I've been looking for you everywhere . . ."*

"Who are you?" Allison said. It was Allison's face, Allison's expression, Allison's unmistakable voice, but she said, *"Who are you, what are you doing here? This is private property, you know!"*

*   *   *

Allison had always been a problem, from the first day when as a girl of five she'd wandered onto the front steps of the Conners' summer cottage at Hunter's Point. No one knew anything about her—where she came from, who her family was, how she happened to appear there. And Allison could remember nothing— not then, not ever.

The Conners had taken her in, of course, and they had been allowed to keep her while the authorities tried without success to trace her family. In time, the Conners had unofficially adopted the little girl and loved her like their own. Which wasn't always easy, for from the beginning she had been difficult, a moody, temperamental child who grew into a defiant, brooding young woman. The Connerses "made allowances."

Perhaps more than anyone else, Peggy Conners made allowances. From the first she had adopted Allison as her younger sister, although there was only two years' difference in their ages. Peggy had always been grownup beyond her years—"A born mother," Mrs. Conners had said of her only child. And Peggy, the born mother, had quickly taken under her wing the moody, withdrawn little sister who had appeared so mysteriously as though in answer to her secret, silent prayer.

"Please, God, bring me a little sister to play with," she had prayed; and just like that, Allison had appeared at the door.

"There's no trace of who she belongs to," the police had said, but Peggy knew, she knew who Allison belonged to; Allison belonged to her.

And, of course, she had spoiled her.

"Just as you're spoiling her now." Mrs. Conners made no secret of her disapproval of Peggy's plan.

"I don't see how you can say that. You told her she couldn't have a trip to Europe, which was what she wanted. All I'm doing is suggesting we spend the summer at the lake, instead. You can't really say she's being spoiled by being given a summer at Hunter's Point in lieu of a summer in Venice or Cannes, or wherever she had her heart set on."

Peggy downed a last swallow of her coffee and came to kiss her mother's cheek. She knew better than to take all this grumbling seriously. For all her stern conversation, Mrs. Conners was a soft-hearted, deeply loving person who, if she hadn't been so sorely tried over the last few years, and if Allison had persisted, probably would have given in on the European trip. Actually, Peggy agreed with her mother; in view of Allison's school record, such a trip would be an extreme indulgence.

"Summer trips are given as rewards," Mrs. Conners said argumentatively, although they both knew the argument was over. "I just can't see rewarding Allison for getting expelled from school. After all, the reason we sent her there—and a private school is expensive, I don't need to remind you—is because she couldn't get along in a public school. And now this, kicked out—if you ask me she needs to spend a summer right here in Columbus, without privileges—"

"Mother, darling, you could no more 'ground' a girl of nineteen today than you could . . ."

"Than I could talk you out of your plans." Her mother sighed. "Very well, do as you think best, but remember, whatever the outcome, this is your idea. Your father seems ready to wash his hands of Allison altogether, and I'm not sure I'd be entirely at odds with that. We've done a great deal for the girl, you can't deny that, and I can't say that she has ever shown the slightest evidence of gratitude . . ."

Peggy had heard all this before and had no need nor desire to hear it again. She set her cup on the kitchen counter, grabbed her purse, and said, "Bye" in the middle of her mother's monologue.

She paused in the hall just long enough to run a comb through her long, dark hair; then she was out of the apartment, on the way to the garage and the battered Jaguar parked there. In a few moments she was cutting in and out of the afternoon traffic, making for the airport.

She was dimly conscious of the admiring glances from men in passing cars, and as usual pleased by it—"Vanity, thy name is Peggy," she teased herself.

She looked forward to the reunion with Allison with mixed feelings. Of course it would be nice to see Allison again; in many ways they had been closer than real sisters would have been. On the other hand, she had no doubt Allison would be in a foul mood, having been refused the summer trip she had wanted. And when Allison was in a bad mood . . . Peggy sighed. If there were a way to avoid trouble, she would find it. But with Allison that was sometimes impossible to do.

She was surprised how Allison had grown up over the year since they had seen each other—not in size, of course, it would be many years now before Allison's slim, petite figure changed much; but the shy, awkward waif had given way to an attractive, determined young woman who strode purposefully toward the gate where Peggy waited. Peggy's own pace, leisurely and graceful, was no match for Allison's swift progress along the corridor.

"It's so good to see you," Peggy said, hurrying to keep up.

"I'm surprised anyone even came for me, I thought I'd been disinherited." Allison's mouth was set in a petulant expression. She tossed her head, sending her blond hair shimmering.

"Oh, Allison, how can you say that? I've even been making plans for the summer, for just the two of us. I thought we'd leave right away for the lake—"

"The lake?" Allison stopped so abruptly that Peggy nearly went on by. "Lake Erie?"

"Well of course Lake Erie. We haven't been there in so long, we can be a couple of little kids again . . ."

Allison began walking again, faster and more determined. "I asked for a trip to Florence and Rome and I end up going to Hunter's Point. It's enough to make me want to turn right around and leave again."

"Why don't you then?" Peggy challenged, feeling stung. Allison threw her a surprised look. "No, seriously," Peggy went on quickly, "if you find the prospect of a few weeks with me so distasteful, you certainly aren't under any pressure to do it. If you'd rather be somewhere else, then go wherever you want."

"And what am I going to go on?" Allison demanded. "Certainly not on the meager allowance the family doles out to me. I've barely been able to meet my school expenses out of that, let alone pay for a trip."

Peggy half opened her mouth to make the expected answer; in the past that sort of remark would have been quite enough to coax her to open her purse; she was always able to set aside a little out of her own allowance and she had never been stingy about sharing it with Allison; but this time her better judgment was in control. Allison had been expelled from school, after all, she had been refused the European trip as a form of punishment; she couldn't satisfy her every whim just to appease her anger. Instinctively Peggy's grip tightened on her purse.

"That isn't fair," she said aloud. "You know you get the same allowance that I get, and you always have."

"Yes, but yours is supplemented; every time you want something, they always come across without a question—of course, you are the *real* daughter, and I'm only an add-on."

Peggy was tempted to reply sharply to the unfair

remark, but they had reached the baggage area and were now surrounded by other passengers waiting for their luggage too. "We'll talk about this when we get to the car," she said firmly. Allison's lower lip moved outward slightly further, but she kept her silence and began to scan the arriving bags, looking for hers—the expensive Vuitton set that the family had given her when she went away, as Peggy was tempted to remind her.

By the time they were in the car, though, Peggy had regained her customary composure. "Look," she said as she headed the Jaguar out of the parking lot, "this trip to the lake isn't mandatory for you, you know. Just because I'm going, you don't have to if you don't want to."

"I thought the law was being laid down." Allison was still petulant. Her long blond hair whipped about her face in the wind. Peggy, who knew that she herself was pretty, had always felt somewhat awed by Allison's loveliness.

"Not in the least. I just thought you'd enjoy being with me at the lake more than you would spending the next few weeks here at the apartment with the folks. But it's really up to you."

There was a long silence while Allison digested that; then, as Peggy had known she would, she sighed and said, "I guess I'll go to the lake with you."

"And I'll guess," Peggy thought wryly, "that this is going to be quite a vacation." But she kept the thought to herself and smiled as she whipped around a Volkswagen in her path. Allison was simply angry now and disappointed in not getting her way. But tomorrow night they would be at the lake, where they'd first met and where they'd shared so many girlhood adventures. Allison would work herself out of the sulks, and when Allison was in a good mood she could be such fun—it would be just like old times.

At least, that was the way Peggy had planned it.

Chapter 2

"The best laid plans," Peggy muttered to herself as she stepped onto the balcony of the little hotel room. Over the tops of the trees she could see the distant waters of the lake, busy now with boats. The sun was sinking toward the horizon and most of the boats were headed in. Behind her, Peggy could hear the sound of the shower running. She was hungry, and hoped Allison didn't linger too long in the bathroom.

It was the better part of a day's drive from Columbus to Hunter's Point, and as the cottage had been closed up so long now, they had decided it would be more practical to spend the night at Hunter's Point's old-fashioned hotel and to tackle putting the cottage in order in the morning.

In fact, Peggy felt more like tackling her adopted sister. Allison's sulky mood had continued unabated throughout the entire journey. She had spoken only to answer Peggy's questions, and then in a petulant, often sarcastic manner. Peggy had begun to feel as if it were she who was being punished for Allison's misbehavior at school.

"Well, this was my own idea," she chided herself.

Behind her she heard Allison, in the bedroom now, rummaging through her luggage. Peggy made herself smile and went back into the room. Allison was holding up a glamorous black dress that must have cost her an entire month's allowance.

"I got this with Paris in mind," she said, tossing it carelessly onto the bed. "I suppose it is a bit *de trop* for Hunter's Point."

"Oh, I don't know, I suppose some of the farm women change from their coveralls before they come in to eat," Peggy said drily. She herself was wearing a flaring denim skirt with huge pockets and a simple checked blouse. She gave Allison an impetuous hug. "Oh, come on, honey, this isn't the end of the world, you know. As long as we're here, why not enjoy outselves?"

"I suppose you're right."

"I know I am—and I'm also starving, and as I recall the food on the terrace is excellent—maybe not Paris or Rome but by provincial standards very good. How about this print number? It's awfully pretty and should be cool."

Although it was a small town, Hunter's Point was a popular resort area and consequently boasted a surprising number of good hotels and restaurants for a town its size. They had often, in the past, come here to the hotel to eat; in addition to the usual coffee shop and a rather overdecorated dining room, there was a really lovely terrace for summer dining, with a view of the lake, overhung with flower-entwined trellises. Peggy had already called down to reserve a table. They were shown to it without delay. While they were scanning the menus, Peggy ordered a bottle of wine; it brought her the first appreciative smile she had gotten so far from Allison.

"I was wondering if you'd get upset if I asked for a drink," she said.

"After all, we *are* grown up now." Peggy said. She sipped the wine and nodded approvingly. "This is good. I don't know if you remember, it comes from around here—near Sandusky."

Allison picked up the bottle and studied the label. "I suppose you chose this because of your astrological sign."

"What do you mean?"

Allison indicated the label; it was dominated by two medieval-looking lions supporting a heraldic banner between them. "Lions—the symbol of Leo," she said. "The House of Lions Fine Wines. I guess I had forgotten that Ohio had a wine district."

"Maybe we should make a tour of the winery," Peggy suggested brightly.

Allison put the bottle down with a thunk. "Somehow I don't think it would measure up to Burgundy or one of the other French wine-growing districts." Allison said unaffably.

"It could, if you'd let it be. But like everything else, if you approach it with your mind already made up that it's going to be a drag, it probably will be."

"Shall we order?" Allison said, obviously wanting to get off the subject.

With that Peggy gave her attention to the menu; they sat in cool silence waiting for their dinner to begin. Finally, too annoyed to care about making a further effort to cheer up Allison, Peggy pushed her chair back from the table.

"Now that the sun's gone it's getting chilly out here. I think I'll get myself a sweater—can I bring you something?"

"No, I'm comfortable, thanks," Allison said.

On her way upstairs in the elevator, though, Peggy regretted having snapped back at Allison. It took two to make a quarrel. After all, this was her vacation, too, and if Allison chose to have a bad time there was no law that said she had to as well. She could go ahead with her own plans and Allison could join her or not as she wished.

When she came back down to the terrace a few minutes later she was surprised to discover that Allison was no longer alone. An older, silver-haired woman had joined her at the table. It had been so many years since they had been to the lake that Peggy was surprised to know Allison had any acquaintances here.

The two at the table were talking animatedly, but as Peggy came across the terrace she saw Allison put a hand gently upon the older woman's hand, and both glanced briefly toward her. For a moment Peggy had the odd impression that Allison had warned the woman of her approach, and their conversation stopped.

"How silly," Peggy quickly chided herself. As she walked up they began talking again.

"It's still cool in the evenings this time of year," the stranger was saying. "Wait a week or so, you'll wish it was like this again."

She turned and smiled up at Peggy as she joined them. "Hello," she said brightly.

"Oh, Peggy, this is Mrs. Denver. There were no tables available and I invited her to join us for a drink—

12

you don't mind, do you?'' Allison seemed to have recovered from her bad mood.

"Not at all." Peggy caught herself before she glanced around at the several empty tables nearby—probably, she told herself, all reserved. "Are you staying here at the hotel too?"

"Yes, for a few days—did you just arrive this evening?" The waitress set a cocktail in front of Mrs. Denver; her question sounded rhetorical to Peggy; surely, in the animated conversation she and Allison had been having, that fact must have already come out.

"Now it's I who am being quarrelsome," Peggy told herself. "It's just Allison's bad mood, rubbed off on me." She smiled and said aloud, "Yes, but we'll only be at the hotel for tonight."

"Oh yes, you have a cottage on the lake, I forgot." Mrs. Denver sipped her drink, her fingers leaving marks on the heavily frosted glass.

She was a strange sort, dressed uniquely enough to seem almost eccentric. Despite the fact that it was evening, she wore a wide-brimmed hat with a veil that did not actually hide but tended to blur her features. She was big boned, and was probably tall, but she sat slumped in her chair, which made it difficult to tell.

"You're a Leo, aren't you?" Mrs. Denver asked unexpectedly.

"Why, yes," Peggy said, surprised for a moment; then she said, "Oh, but Allison must have said something to you."

"No need, it's obvious at a glance. The stateliness of bearing, the firm step, the Roman features, even the deliberation in the way you speak. No, my dear, I needn't be told, I could see at a glance that you are the proud royal sign."

Despite herself Peggy found that she responded pleasurably to the flattery. She had never really given any credence to the so-called science of astrology, but Mrs. Denver's observations certainly were intriguing. Had she really guessed her sign correctly, or had Allison told her? Allison certainly wasn't letting the cat out of the bag if that were so.

The waitress arrived then with entrées for Peggy and Allison and the conversation dwindled to small talk. The food was good and Peggy was ravenous—the lake always seemed to perk up her appetite. Mrs. Denver and Allison continued to talk about astrology; Mrs. Denver seemed quite knowledgeable on the subject. To Peggy's surprise, so did Allison, who had never really discussed it with her before.

Peggy's chair was facing the door and as she glanced up she saw a man standing in the doorway staring at their table. He was huge, tall and thickly built, with coarse features that seemed set in a permanent scowl. An involuntary shiver ran up Peggy's spine.

Mrs. Denver, noticing the movement, followed Peggy's glance toward the doorway. "Oh, that's Waldo, my chauffeur, I'm afraid I must go." She finished her cocktail and pushed her chair back, standing. "It's been so pleasant talking with you both. I hope we meet again."

"I'm sure we shall," Allison said.

Peggy watched the older woman cross the terrace. She moved gracefully; her walk, her dress, the authentic glimmer of her jewelry, spoke of breeding, class, wealth. Yet there was something about her that jarred

14

—Peggy could not quite put her finger on it. She watched Mrs. Denver and her brutish-looking chauffeur speak to each other for a moment. Suddenly they both glanced back at the table where Peggy was sitting, and for the briefest fraction of a second Peggy's eyes met those of the chauffeur. It sent another shiver along her spine. Mrs. Denver said something to him then and walked away, and the big man followed her.

"Now that's a strange pair," Peggy said, sipping her coffee.

"Mrs. Denver? I thought she was very charming. Of course I didn't get a look at the chauffeur—what was his name, Walter?"

"Waldo—and lucky you. How about a stroll down to the landing?"

"Hmm? Oh, okay."

It had seemed to Peggy while Mrs. Denver was at the table that Allison had quite recovered from her previous mood, but now, as they strolled along the darkening streets, Allison seemed to withdraw into herself. She was thoughtful and uncommunicative, as if entirely wrapped up in some private consideration, and at length, despairing of any sort of companionship, Peggy announced that after all she was tired from the long drive, and perhaps they should just call it a day and get an early start the next morning setting the cottage in order.

It did not take long to put the cottage in order. Dust covers had to be removed and the rooms needed a quick run-through with the vacuum cleaner. They had called ahead to have the utilities turned on and by midmorning things were relatively shipshape.

"That's about everything except the shopping," Peggy announced. "Let's get that out of the way before lunch, okay?"

Allison had apparently gotten over her sulks, but her private, withdrawn mood from the night before had continued. All morning long, while she had worked about the cottage, she had acted as if she were wrestling with some problem of her own.

"Why don't you go ahead," Allison said, "there're one or two things I'd like to do around here."

"Look, there isn't something new bothering you, is there? Something you want to talk about?"

Allison shook her head. "No, not really. You go ahead, don't worry about me."

For a moment Peggy was tempted to push the subject; then she thought better of it. "Okay. See you in about an hour."

She drove into the village, parking the car in the municipal lot, and walked around to do her errands. The phone still hadn't been connected, so she had to pay a visit to the phone company, and there were myriad things to be purchased at the five and dime—a new cord for the electric percolator, the previous one seemingly having disappeared, plus pins and needles and threads, a couple of odd cooking utensils to replace old ones that had been discarded or transported back to Columbus in the past—the paraphernalia of summer resort living.

"That shop looks new," she thought on her way back to the car, her arms laden with little packages. A sign over the window, done in garish, hand-drawn letters, identified the shop as The Black Candle, and smaller lettering went on to inform that they specialized in the occult. Peggy paused for a glance at the display window—it was all tarot cards, candles of every size and description, Ouija boards, glass spheres that she decided must be intended as crystal balls, all a bit artificial and pretentious, but very popular these days.

She was about to walk on when she realized that the lone customer in the shop, talking with the salesgirl, was Mrs. Denver. It seemed to be a very intense conversation and Peggy found herself remembering Mrs. Denver's interest in astrology. No doubt she was guessing the girl's astrological sign and explaining how she knew.

Smiling to herself, Peggy went on to the car, piled her packages in the back seat, and drove to the market. It was nearly noon by the time she headed for home, the little car now filled with bags and packages. The weather had turned warm and she was looking forward to dispensing with chores and enjoying her vacation. The boat, kept in storage, had been cleaned and serviced for them, and was waiting at the dock. It would be a great afternoon for boating.

Her route took her again past the boat landing, busy now with tourist traffic. She liked the bustle, the smell of fresh fish and the roar of boats and voices and cars. She was sitting at a red light, admiring the activity, when she suddenly saw Mrs. Denver again, and with her, of all people, Allison. The two of them were walking along side by side, talking with their heads bent close. At the moment Allison seemed very engrossed in something Mrs. Denver was saying.

Peggy would have honked and tried to wave them over to the car but at first she was too surprised at seeing Allison there, and by the time she had collected her wits, the light had changed. She drove off slowly, watching them in the rear-view mirror until they were out of sight.

She realized the incident troubled her out of all proportion. Of course it was only a trivial thing, of course she was being unreasonable in having taken such an immediate dislike—no, distrust was more the word—to Mrs. Denver. It was all very silly and point-less. But why on earth had Allison told her that she wanted to do some things around the cottage if what she really intended to do was meet Mrs. Denver? It was not as if Allison had to have her permission to strike up a friendship. It seemed so . . . Peggy hesitated . . . sneaky.

"On the other hand," she reasoned, "there's nothing to say she actually intended meeting Mrs. Denver. Maybe I'm flying off the handle."

By the time Allison returned to the cottage, lunch was nearly ready. Peggy, working in the kitchen, heard the front screen door bang shut and made a mental note that they needed a new spring for it.

"Hi," Allison said amiably, coming into the kitchen. She was dressed neatly—not as if she were just relaxing at a lake resort town, but dressed up—as if she had had a business appointment, Peggy found herself thinking.

"Hi yourself—I thought you were going to stick around here?"

"Oh, I was, but I got restless, so I decided to go for a stroll along the landing. It was kind of nice, really. I guess I'd forgotten that Hunter's Point is such a pretty little town."

Peggy, waiting for Allison to volunteer the information that she had run into Mrs. Denver, realized as the silence grew that it was not forthcoming. She almost asked, "Meet anyone?" but checked herself at the last minute. Allison looked so happy, so recovered from her moods, that she hated to spoil it by sounding as though she'd been checking up on her.

"You know, I haven't been very good company so far," Allison said, coming up behind her and putting an arm about Peggy's shoulders, "and I *am* sorry, Peg. I promise you won't have to put up with any more of my bad moods."

And after that Peggy could not ask about Mrs. Denver at all.

Chapter 3

They ate at the hotel again that evening, at Allison's suggestion. "After spending the afternoon out in the boat, I just can't see sweating over a hot stove," was how she had put it, and at first Peggy had expected Mrs. Denver to show up "spontaneously" at their table. But as the meal progressed and no one appeared, Peggy began to relax and, for the first time this trip, to enjoy Allison's company.

"Something's certainly gotten into you," she said over dessert. "Ever since I picked you up at the airport you've been on a gloom trip and today you're looking like the cat that swallowed the canary. How about telling me what's up?"

Allison smiled mysteriously. "You wouldn't understand if I did."

"Try me."

"Mercury is in perigee." Allison's eyes twinkled with a mischievous light. She looked all at once like the little girl who used to teasingly hide Peggy's dolls.

"Mercury . . . What on earth is that supposed to mean? Peri . . . what did you call it?"

Allison shrugged. "I told you you wouldn't understand it."

"But . . ."

Allison pushed her chair back, laughing. "Come on, let's stroll back to the house. I'm for calling it a night."

"Already? But it's only eight-thirty. And anyway, I want to know what you meant about Mercury in whatever it was."

"It may only be eight-thirty but it's been a long, active day and I plan on bedding down. And as for the other, don't worry yourself about it, you'll understand better tomorrow."

"Some sort of surprise?"

They came out of the restaurant onto the darkening street and turned toward the cottage. "Exactly."

Peggy stole a sideways glance at Allison. She looked so keyed up, so exhilarated, that for a moment Peggy had a pang of doubt—there was so much that she didn't know or understand about her sister. Was there some unsavory explanation for these sudden and drastic changes of mood?

"I'm really never satisfied," she scolded herself silently. "I'm unhappy when she's in a bad mood and when she gets herself out of it, I'm still not happy." She resolved to be patient and wait until morning to learn what Allison's secret was; whatever it was, it had certainly lifted Allison's spirits, and maybe it would do as much for hers.

The cottage was at the end of a shady street; there were other cottages along this way, but at the time only one other one, about half a block up from theirs, was occupied. A distorted rectangle of light spilled from its window across the sidewalk.

"I wonder who that is," Peggy said.

"Who?"

"That car—a Rolls-Royce, yet, parked down by our place." She nodded toward the large silvery car parked—or so it seemed from that distance—directly in front of their cottage.

Allison shrugged. "Probably another of the summer residents."

"But none of the other cottages is opened up yet— oh, it's leaving."

As she spoke the Rolls began to glide silently away from the curb, in their direction. A moment later it passed them. Peggy did a double take; she had had only a quick glimpse of the driver before he had turned his head, but she would have sworn it was Mrs. Denver's chauffeur—what had his name been, Waldo—and that shadowy figure in the back seat, leaning far back into the corner had that been . . . ?

"Did you recognize them?" she asked.

"Who?" Allison gave her a blank look.

"In that car, I would have sworn it was Waldo and Mrs. Denver."

"I didn't see them. But maybe it was. Maybe Mrs. Denver got lonesome for some company and decided to look us up. From the way she talked I got the feeling she doesn't know anyone here and I'd say she's the sort who meets people slowly."

"I would have said she was rather forward about meeting people," Peggy disagreed, remembering the way Mrs. Denver had joined them at their table the night before. "And at any rate, they just drove right by us. If they had been looking for us, don't you think they would have recognized us?"

"Well then, there you have it, they couldn't have been looking for us. When you get right down to it, it's kind of flattering ourselves to think she'd even remember us after one meeting, let alone look us up. She was probably trying to find someone else who lives down this way."

"But . . ."

"Oh, look. Sis, why don't we just drop it?" There was a note of sharpness in Allison's voice, and Peggy restrained her questions. She didn't want to ruin Allison's good mood now that she was finally perking up. Perhaps Mrs. Denver had something to do with Allison's surprise for the morning and that was why Allison was being so mysterious and secretive. Yes, now that she thought of it, that was a likely explanation. Perhaps Mrs. Denver had delivered something for Allison while they were out, something Allison didn't want Peggy to see yet—although certainly Mrs. Denver was the most unlikely delivery person Peggy could think of.

"I suppose you're right," she said, impulsively linking her arm through Allison's as they crossed the street. But she couldn't resist a quick glance over her shoulder. The street was now silently empty, not even the purr of a distant motor could be heard to prove that a car had ever been there.

It was the sound of a car that roused Peggy from her bed much later, in the middle of the night. For some minutes she had been lying awake, staring up at the ceiling. Something had awakened her, she couldn't say with certainty just what, some sound, a door closing perhaps. She had been lying there listening for a repetition of it, wondering if she should get up and go investigate. There had been nothing for several minutes and then, faintly, the sound of a car door, and an engine coming to life.

She kicked back the light blanket and got out of bed, the floor cold on her bare feet. The bedrooms were in the rear, looking down toward the lake; the living room and kitchen were on the street side of the house, so that she had to walk the width of the house to reach one of the windows looking out onto the street. By that time the car that she'd heard was gone; she had just a glimpse of red taillights disappearing in the distance.

"Just some kids, out parking," she told herself, letting the curtains flutter closed.

But she felt a strange prickling of uneasiness. Certain that she would not go easily back to sleep, she went into the kitchen and poured herself a glass of milk. She was seated at the little kitchen table, sipping it and feeling wide awake, when the rain began to fall, a gentle tapping at the window. Remembering the open window by her bed, she hurried back to her bedroom to close it.

"May as well get Allison's too," she thought, and stole into Allison's room on tiptoe.

She had closed the window and was almost to the hall again when she sensed something odd about Allison's room.

"Allison?" she whispered. She moved closer to the bed.

It was empty.

"Allison?" She flicked on the lamp beside the bed, blinking in its sudden glare, and looked around. Allison was not in the room. "Where are you?" she called louder.

She went through the cottage, turning on lights, and

as she went her uneasiness of a few minutes ago began to grow into genuine anxiety. The clock on the kitchen wall informed her it was ten minutes of four in the morning. Where on earth could Allison be at that hour?

She remembered the car she had heard. What if it had been her car, she thought suddenly, and hurried through the door that connected kitchen with garage. No, hers was just where she had left it. Anyway, she ought to have known hers would have made a great deal more noise; the one she heard had been very quiet, a purr almost—like a Rolls-Royce. The thought came unbidden into her mind.

"Wait a minute, let's not panic," she said aloud. Her voice sounded odd in the predawn stillness of the empty cottage. For all she knew, Allison had acquired a habit of middle-of-the-night strolls.

Peggy made herself a cup of tea and sat in the kitchen sipping it thoughtfully, trying not to glance at the clock every minute or two. Finally, thinking that if Allison should come in she might think Peggy was waiting up to check on her, she went back to her bedroom and crawled into bed. Perhaps, she reasoned, Allison had met a boy and made a date—but so late? And why make a secret of it? Certainly she knew Peggy wouldn't object to her dating. Or *did* she know that? Perhaps she really had gotten the idea that she was being punished, and that part of that punishment was a restriction of her freedom.

"I'll have to straighten that out in the morning," Peggy told herself firmly. If—and she was sorry at once that she had let this thought into her consciousness—if Allison were home in the morning.

Chapter 4

Allison was not home by morning and Peggy, weary
from lack of sleep and from worrying, made another
discovery that had been overlooked during the night.
Not only was Allison gone, but all her belongings were
gone too. Her closet and dresser were empty, her bags
missing. There wasn't a trace of her in the room or, but
for an empty coffee cup on the kitchen counter, anywhere in the cottage.

Peggy made herself coffee and sat deliberately contemplating the singular situation in which she found
herself. Where, she asked herself again and again, had
Allison gone? And why? Aside from her sulks at the
beginning there was no reason for her to disappear, and
by yesterday she had seemed to work herself out of her
moods. She had been great fun yesterday on the boat,
and again at dinner last night. The only time she had
shown any sharpness had been on their way home,
when Peggy thought she had seen Mrs. Denver, in that
car . . . At once Peggy's thoughts went to the sound of
a car door shutting in the wee hours, when she had been
lying awake, and the quiet murmur of an engine. Mrs.
Denver, parked outside their cottage during the eve-

ning; Mrs. Denver, mysteriously joining them at the dinner table, thrusting herself into their lives; Mrs. Denver mysteriously meeting Allison during the afternoon.

Peggy could not shake her growing conviction that Mrs. Denver was the key to Allison's sudden disappearance. She was now certain that Mrs. Denver was with Allison, or if she wasn't, would know where Allison was.

Peggy pushed aside her half-finished cup of coffee and, dressing hurriedly, left for the police station downtown.

The officer she talked to, however, did not seem particularly impressed with Allison's disappearance. He filled out a report, asking Peggy questions in what seemed to her an uninterested voice.

"The missing girl is your sister, you say?" His pen moved rapidly over the official-looking paper.

"Yes—adopted sister, actually." She wished he would look up at her, show some concern or sympathy—anything but this complete lack of interest.

"And she ran off, you think?"

"I don't—no, I don't think she just 'ran off'—I don't know what happened to her. That's what I want you to find out."

He did look up then, studying her in a businesslike way. "How old is your sister—excuse me, adopted sister?"

"She's nineteen."

He laid the pen down and leaned back in his chair, folding his hands in front of him. "You understand, legally this girl is an adult, she can come and go as she pleases?''

Peggy took a deep breath; this man annoyed her—he was so unconcerned, so stickling, when all the while Allison was . . . whatever Allison was. ''Yes, of course, I understand that, but if she didn't go of her own accord. . . ?''

That roused him a little. He leaned forward again, but he did not pick up his pen. ''You think there's something fishy about her leaving?''

She managed something of a smile for the officer for the first time since she had come in. Finally she had his interest. ''Yes, I do,'' she said firmly.

''This room she left, was there any sign of a struggle?''

''Why, no, but . . .'' She had lost him again; he leaned back, the chair squeaking. ''I can't imagine she would just voluntarily sneak away in the middle of the night. As you said, she is an adult, there would be no reason to run away.''

He narrowed his eyes. ''You two had any kind of quarrel?''

She hesitated, but she saw from his expression that he had noted her reaction to the question, and already guessed the answer. ''Yes, we did, earlier, but it was all patched up. Really, it was; she was fine yesterday.''

He was nodding his head knowingly. She felt like stamping her foot or shouting, anything to get through to him. ''And she gave you no clue that anything was going to happen, that she had anything in mind?''

Like an unwelcome guest the memory came back to her; in all her concern she had forgotten it until now.

Her face reddened as she said, "Well, she did say she had a surprise for me, for this morning—but I'm sure she didn't mean . . ." She stopped. As she had realized he would, he had already drawn his own conclusions. He spread his hands out flat.

"There you have it. Her surprise was that she had some plans of her own. Maybe she eloped . . ."

"By herself? She didn't know anyone here."

The officer went on, oblivious to her interruption. "You told me earlier you'd seen her talking to some woman, Denver, was that it? Maybe she had more friends around than you knew. Maybe a boyfriend followed her up here from school. Maybe she just felt like being by herself."

Angrily, Peggy said, "In other words, you don't intend to do anything to find her?"

He sighed. "Miss, there is nothing I can do. A legal adult decides to leave, there's no evidence of a struggle, apparently she left of her own volition. It happens all the time. Look, I'll tell you what, if it'll make you happier I'll send someone around to the cottage, to have a look around. Maybe—I doubt it, but just maybe—your sister was taken against her will and someone took the time to straighten things around neatly—you have to admit, it sounds unlikely, with you sleeping in the next room. But I'll have one of our men check it out, okay?"

"And in the meantime there's no way you can look for her? She *is* a missing person, isn't she?"

"Not legally, not until she's been missing for twenty-four hours. If you want to come back tomorrow and file a missing persons report, well . . ." His shrug said that he didn't think it would be worth her while.

Peggy bit her lip in frustration. She tried to think of something she could say that would change his mind. Finally, unable to think of anything more, she turned on her heel and started away.

"Miss, take my advice, don't worry about it," he called after her, "I'd be willing to bet money that by this time tomorrow you'll know where she is."

She paused to look over her shoulder. "That might not necessarily be a blessing," she said.

Outside she hesitated indecisively. Of course there was always the possibility he was right, that Allison had gone freely—not to elope, certainly, there would have been some clue or hint of that. A joke perhaps? What was it she had said last night—Mercury was in . . . she searched for the word . . . Mercury was in perigee. What on earth could it mean? It sounded like astrology—Mercury was a planet, and she vaguely thought she remembered one of her girl friends, who went in for astrology, talking about Mercury in her horoscope.

And astrology brought her right back to Mrs. Denver. Peggy was more convinced than ever that Mrs. Denver was the key to the mystery. She glanced down the street; the hotel was only a few blocks from here. Had Mrs. Denver said she was staying at the hotel, or had she only been there that evening for cocktails?

She felt that doing anything was better than doing nothing, and walked down to the hotel. She was known to the desk clerk, which made her task a little easier, but not much more fruitful.

"Mrs. Denver—yes, she was here, but she checked out this morning," he said, looking through registration cards. "During the night, actually. It was before I came on, at five. Unusual time to check out. She must have had a long trip ahead of her.''

''Or some other reason for such an odd hour,'' Peggy said. She was not really surprised at all that Mrs. Denver had disappeared along with Allison.

''Look, do you have an address for her, a home address?''

He scowled. ''I'm afraid we're not allowed to give out that information,'' he said. ''You can understand—invasion of privacy, that sort of thing.''

''Yes, of course,'' she said, disappointed nonetheless.

She was almost back to her car, parked by the police station, when she again passed the shop she had noticed the day before, The Black Candle. She paused to gaze inside. A young girl with a long ponytail was just opening up for the day. On an impulse Peggy went inside.

''Hello, can I help you?'' The girl gave her a friendly smile.

''Perhaps,'' Peggy began, feeling a little foolish. ''I—I'm looking for someone. I thought you might have some idea where I could find her.''

The girl shrugged; her expression seemed to say ''this isn't going to make me any money.'' But she said politely enough, ''I'm new in town, I'm afraid I don't know very many people around here. What was the name?''

''Her name is Denver, Mrs. Denver. She's an older woman, about fifty I should say, silver-gray hair, and very knowledgeable about astrology. I saw her in here yesterday talking to you.''

"Yes, she didn't give me her name, but I do remember a woman who looked like that. She stopped by in the morning." The girl's eyes narrowed suspiciously. "What did you say you wanted to find her for?"

"I—we shared a table at the restaurant last night and she gave me a lift home afterward," Peggy swiftly lied, "but I seem to have left my sweater in her car—it was an expensive sweater, you see, cashmere—but I couldn't remember where she said she was staying, and then when I came by here I remembered she had been here. She didn't say where she was from or anything, did she?"

"No, but you can make a swap if you want, because she left something here." The girl went behind the counter and reached down, bringing up a cigarette case and a book of matches. "Not exactly a cashmere sweater, but I suppose it'll make up a little for the loss. Anyway, I don't smoke, so you may as well have them."

"Oh—thank you." Peggy picked up the case and matches. "Perhaps I can find her and return these—as well as retrieve my sweater."

"Good luck, but I don't think she was from around here."

Peggy wasn't listening; she was staring down at the items in her hand. The case was an expensive one, alligator trimmed in gold; but it was the matches that interested her. They had come from a bank in Ives. Ives Point was near Sandusky along the lake shore, and the heart of Ohio's grape-growing region. The Ives ferry carried passengers to the offshore islands—Middle Bass, Put-in-Bay, and several smaller, privately owned islands—on which were the chief vineyards and wineries of the area.

She turned the matchbook over in her hand. Banks often printed their advertising on matchbooks but they did not as a rule distribute them anywhere but in their own banks. If Mrs. Denver had had these matches in her possession, she had either gotten them from someone who had been in that bank, or she had been in the bank herself.

While she had been studying the matches a customer had come into the shop, and the girl was now busy with her. Thinking of something else she wanted to ask, Peggy lingered, waiting for her to be free again. She strolled around, looking at the merchandise. On a rack was a series of books devoted to astrology, one book for each of the twelve zodiac signs. On an impulse she picked up the book on Leo and skimmed through its pages.

"The Leo woman is vain, egotistical," she read, "Somewhat lazy at times . . . graceful, but leisurely in movement, vulnerable to flattery. She tends to have dark eyes and full, flowing hair. Vanity is the key . . ."

"What foolishness," she thought, replacing the book on the rack. She turned and as she did so caught a glimpse of herself in an ornate mirror on one wall; she saw, as if for the first time, her large brown eyes and great mane of hair, and thought of the pleasure she took when people looked admiringly at her. She could not help laughing at herself, a welcome change of feeling from the worrying mood she had been in all morning. She decided after all that she should buy something to make up for using so much of the salesgirl's time, and retrieved the astrology book.

At last the salesgirl was free again and reestablished behind the counter. Peggy walked over to her, laying the book down and with it the money to cover its cost.

"I wonder," she said as the girl rang up the sale, "You seem to know astrology, could you help me with something?"

"I'll try, but I'm not in a class with your friend—she was uncanny. I would have liked her to cast my chart."

"If someone said to you, 'Mercury is in perigee'—I think that's the right phrase but I'm not certain—what would it mean?"

The girl frowned as she put the book and sales slip into a bag. "Well, I'm not sure exactly. Perigee is an astronomical term, it means a planet or a heavenly body is at its closest point to the earth—in other words, Mercury is as close to earth as it ever gets."

"Yes, but what does that mean astrologically? Has it any special significance?"

"I don't know specifically about Mercury, but when a planet is closest to earth—in perigee—it means that it has its strongest influence. And Mercury . . . let me see . . . Mercury is an important body. It influences moods, for one thing—you know, people who have wild ups and then wild downs—Mercury moods, a friend of mine calls them, and does he suffer from them! You never know what he's going to do next. I guess if Mercury was in perigee, he'd be likely to do anything, you know, jump from the Empire State Building, race a train, wrestle tigers. It's an energy sign, for one thing, and a sign of variety. Is your friend a Gemini? They're awfully influenced by Mercury. And another thing, Mercury people are influenced by the people around them. And they desire change. Does any of that help?''

"I'm not sure," Peggy said. "Let me see, you mean that if Mercury is in perigee, all of these influences would be heightened, right?''

"Exactly. Anybody who's a Mercury person would be just—like spaced out, if you know what I mean. I mean, they're liable to jump at just any harebrained idea.''

Peggy smiled wryly and nodded. "Yes, I think that about covers it. Thanks again.''

"Any time.'' The clerk's quick, shallow smile slid from Peggy to a new customer who had just entered the shop. This time Peggy left. She retrieved her car from the station and drove thoughtfully home to the cottage. Its rooms seemed to echo eerily as she let herself in.

Mercury in perigee. Allison, looking like the cat who swallowed the canary, and then disappearing during the night, not a word, not a trace. Had Allison dropped that teasing morsel as an explanation—or a clue? What could it possibly mean? Was she off on some lark? Or was she in some kind of trouble?

"And what do I do about the folks?'' Peggy wondered aloud, once more surveying Allison's empty bedroom. She dreaded the thought of calling home and informing them of yet another problem with Allison. Her father had warned that he was at the end of his patience with Allison's antics; even if this proved to be some sort of innocent escapade, it just might be the straw that breaks the camel's back.

"But what if it isn't innocent?'' That was the question that continued to haunt her. Allison was impulsive, quick to jump into things—often foolish, even dangerous things. What kind of situation might she have gotten into now?

One thing was for certain, Mrs. Denver was no foolish schoolgirl. Peggy had the conviction that whatever Mrs. Denver might be involved in was deadly serious.

She took the cigarette case and matchbook from her purse and studied them again. Ives. An hour's drive along the lake. Of course, there was no assurance she would be able to find Allison, or even Mrs. Denver there. She had only a book of matches to hint that either of them had even gone in that direction.

On the other hand, it was the only clue she had.

It was worth a try. She went into her bedroom and began tossing things into an overnight bag.

Chapter 5

"And not much of a clue," she thought later, staring at the ferry that carried cars and passengers from Ives Point to Put-in-Bay. The next boat left at 2:45—thirty minutes from now, and in the next fifteen minutes she must decide whether to put her car in the already growing line of waiting cars. From Ives Point the ferry made a fifteen-minute trip to the Lime Kiln Docks and from there, she had been informed, it was just a mile and a half into the main part of town at Put-in-Bay.

But exactly what, she wondered, would she accomplish by reaching the main part of town? Or, for that matter, what had she accomplished by coming this far?

She had found the bank from which the matches had come, but once there she found herself at a dead end. She had even talked to a teller, who knew no one named Denver, and who had explained that she was not at liberty to give out information regarding customers, although she was persuaded—perhaps by Peggy's expression of innocence—to check. Alas, there was no "Denver" account on file.

Short of waiting in the bank's lobby for days until—

and if—Mrs. Denver showed up, there seemed really nothing more Peggy could do.

She gave a sigh of discouragement and dropped onto a wooden bench along the sidewalk. It was no use, she might well go back to Hunter's Point and call the family; perhaps they could suggest a next step. At least she wouldn't feel so all alone in this.

It was at this low point in her search that chance again favored her. She glanced toward the ferry, still debating whether to make the trip across to Put-in-Bay, and saw a familiar, hulking figure—Waldo, Mrs. Denver's chauffeur walking rapidly along the boat landing.

Her heart leapt up. Then she had been right in letting the matchbook lead her here—if Waldo was here, could Mrs. Denver be far behind?

She jumped up and started after him, but the traffic held her back for a moment and by the time she had crossed to where he had been he was gone from sight. This was a popular tourist point and there were crowds of people everywhere, some waiting for the ferry, others just strolling about.

She hurried along in the direction he had taken, looking right and left. Surely he couldn't have just disappeared? And yet it seemed that he had, for there was no sight of him anywhere.

Now wait a minute, she thought, halting. This was broad daylight, all around her were people, movement, the sights and sounds and smells of a boat landing. Gulls wheeled and cried, children yelled, somewhere nearby an engine sprang into life.

She turned to retrace her steps. As she did so a boat slipped from its mooring. The movement caught her eye and she turned toward it in time to see the brutish

Waldo at the wheel of a powerful inboard cruiser. Even as she watched the boat accelerated, the nose lifting slightly, and moved away from the landing.

She walked to the dock where it had been moored, staring after it in frustration as the boat, moving ever more swiftly, shrank in the distance. An old man who had been fishing from the dock nearby was gathering up his things. He had the look of a local rather than a tourist, and on an impulse she went up to him.

"Excuse me," she said, giving him a hopeful smile, "Do you know that boat that just left?"

He glanced over the water briefly, then back at her. "Reckon I do," he said laconically.

"Can you tell me who it belongs to?"

"Belongs to the Lions family. This is their dock. What do you want to know for?"

"I—I thought I knew that man who was just driving it now." She tried to make her inquiries sound casual, not too concerned, but hope was rising like a mountain spring within her.

"That'd be Waldo."

"Yes, that's him," she said, unable to keep from sounding pleased. "Where—where could I find him if I wanted to see him again?"

His look questioned why anyone would want to see Waldo again, but he simply said, "He works for the family, reckon you'd have to go there." He nodded his head toward the water.

"They live on the lake somewhere?"

"Not on it, in it, so to speak. Lions Island, straight out there, beyond Sugar and Rattlesnake Islands. It's where the wine is made."

The name registered with her then: Lions. The

House of Lions. Ohio's premier wine. She had read once of their island vineyards, supposedly the finest Catawba vineyards in the country.

"Of course, how stupid of me," she murmured. "Is the island on one of the tours?"

He snorted at the foolishness of her question. "Lions Island? Not likely. They don't encourage any kind of visitors. Afraid someone would step on a grape, most likely. Look, little lady, I don't know what your interest in the Lionses is, but if I was you I'd forget it. The last fellow tried to visit out there got thrown into the lake, clothes and all, liked to drown before he got back to his boat. Why don't you take one of the regular tours, there're plenty of wineries you can visit with no trouble, and forget you ever saw this Waldo fellow. Maybe it ain't for me to say, but that one's a mean customer, he ain't for the likes of you."

Peggy stared out over the water, her mind filled with her own confused thoughts. Waldo. Allison. Mrs. Denver. A mysterious island somewhere in the lake, a famed family of vintners. She did not understand how, but she knew that somehow it all tied together. It was like a siren's song, calling her to Lions Island.

"Is there somewhere I can rent a boat?" she asked finally.

The old man's eyes said all: He knew her for a fool. But at last he shrugged and said, "Old George, two docks down, he's got the best ones to rent." He collected his gear and, plainly dismissing her and her problems from his mind, shuffled away, shaking his head.

The island lay like a green cloud on the watery

horizon. It had been easy to find with Old George's directions, although he too had regarded her as more than a little crazy, and had demanded twice the usual deposit on the boat.

"Never know if I'm going to get it back, you going out there," he said.

"But why, what's the big bugaboo about going to Lions Island?" she had asked.

He was no more informative than the old fisherman had been, though. "They don't like visitors," was all he said.

"Well, you don't have to worry about your boat. I'm quite used to handling one, and I promise I only intend to see someone at the house and talk to them a few minutes."

"You'll never get past the gates. No one ever does. Guarded by lions, they say."

She had felt a shiver of apprehension then. "Lions? You mean real ones? Surely they don't have dangerous animals roaming loose on the island?"

He had fixed his eyes on hers and said, "Take my advice, head for Put-in-Bay, have yourself something to eat—try Daisy's, it ain't much to look at but the food's damned good—and then head back here."

The island grew larger, until its features were distinct. It was so little known or publicized that in her mind she had pictured it as small, but now she could see it was not, it looked as large as the larger islands in the chain. She could see the slopes, planted with vines, and in the distance, apparently on the middle of the island, the house, a grand old chateaulike manor. And around it all, encircling the entire island, was a forbidding stone wall. She reflected on the work that must have

43

gone into transporting all that stone to an island in the middle of a lake. Even from the first, the Lions family must have valued their privacy very highly.

She spotted a landing with a boathouse as elegant as many fine homes. She headed for it, cutting back the engine; it was foolish to suppose she could just arrive and stroll up to the house unnoticed, but she felt an instinctive urge to be as quiet about her arrival as possible.

As it was, no one seemed to notice her as she landed. She docked, tied up the boat, and scrambled up onto the dock. Still she saw no one. In the boathouse, she had had a glimpse of the cruiser she had seen Waldo piloting.

The stone wall came almost down to the dock, and there, directly before her, was a great iron gate, barring her way. Of course, she should have realized, treasuring their isolation as they did, the Lionses would not have left it possible for anyone who did stop uninvited at their dock to simply come up to the house. But there must be some way for visitors to announce their arrival, a bell or something. She looked and saw the bell, but she did not ring it at once. Beyond the gates were a gravel drive and a small cultivated forest. From here the wall was too high for her to see over, and the trees effectively hid the house from any curious eyes.

Then, she suddenly saw the lions. Massive iron beasts that seemed poised to strike.

This was the moment that was to haunt Peggy again and again, as if in a constantly-recurring dream. Where was Allison? Was she behind the grim, forbidding gate of the lions? Or was this a wild goose chase; had Allison simply disappeared on a puff of smoke?

44

Peggy stared at the great iron lions crouched on either side, guarding the gates of the estate ahead of her. Lions were her symbol, she had learned, symbol of the sign Leo. But these were not the warm, friendly lions always pictured to represent the astrological Leo. They were fierce and angry looking, and they seemed a warning of violence and tragedy to anyone who dared pass beyond them. They seemed to intimidate as effectively as living lions would have done.

Peggy reached out and put a hand on the wrought iron of one gate. It swung inward at her touch. It was not locked after all. Perhaps the owners thought the sight of their massive structure and their leonine guards, were enough to discourage trespassers. Under most circumstances, Peggy thought, they surely would be. For a moment, no more, she hesitated. Then she passed through, casting an apprehensive glance up at one of the beasts.

Beware, we stand at the gates of hell, was the inscription above the gate. It was carved into the stone, in letters so bold that they seemed almost to speak their warning aloud.

She was inside, standing in the drive that led through the trees. The family apparently drove from house to dock; she had estimated the island's width to be two miles, perhaps more, so it would indeed have been a long walk.

A sudden sound in the shrubbery to her right made her start. She turned, and to her amazement there was Allison, the leaves of a tree casting shadows across her pale face—but it was Allison, unmistakably Allison. A flood of relief rushed over Peggy.

"Allison, thank God I've found you," Peggy cried.

"What on earth has happened to you? I've been look-ing everywhere for you . . ."

"Who are you?" Allison asked.

Peggy stood stunned into silence, unable to believe what she had heard. She stared at the girl before her. It was Allison's face, Allison's expression, Allison's voice. But it was the soul of a stranger who was saying, "Who are you, what are you doing here? This is private property, you know. We don't allow trespassers."

Chapter 6

Peggy, still speechless, could only stare at the angry-looking person before her. She even doubted her own senses—could she have made a mistake? Was it only someone who looked like Allison, a resemblance magnified by her concern for her missing sister? She was certain she had never seen Allison in that outfit—jodhpurs, a silk blouse that most certainly came straight from Paris, a Hermes scarf—she looked elegant, poised, the mistress of her world.

Peggy shook her head as if to dislodge her confusing thoughts. No, it had to be Allison. There couldn't be two people who looked that much alike, even to Allison's way of cocking her head slightly to the side when she looked directly at you.

''Why are you staring at me like that?'' Allison demanded. ''And why haven't you answered any of my questions? You'd better talk fast, before I summon the servants and have you thrown back into the lake.''

The cold arrogance of these remarks finally penetrated Peggy's confusion, replacing her bewilderment with anger. She'd been through a dreadful scare; her holiday had been ruined. She had had to boat out to this island, only to find Allison apparently caught up in a weird drama of her own making—and treating her as though she were a criminal.

"How dare you," she said angrily, taking a step closer to Allison, "after all you've put me through. I ought to grab you and shake a little sense into you, of all the stupid things you've ever done, this is far and away the most—"

"What's going on here?"

Peggy jumped and whirled about; she had become so excited about finding Allison, and then so angry at Allison's behavior, that she had been unaware anyone else was approaching down the gravel drive. Now the man was directly behind her, and he looked no more friendly or welcoming than Allison.

"What is this all about?" he demanded again, fixing steel gray eyes on Peggy. They were cold eyes, and hard; one could not imagine them ever lighting up with pleasure, or happiness; certainly not with kindness or love. He was tall and handsome, but his mouth was a cruel, sensuous line. Even his dark hair seemed spoiled, spilling in willful, undisciplined curls across his bronze forehead.

"A trespasser, Alex," Allison said, speaking past Peggy. "I found her sneaking around down here and ordered her off the island, but she refuses to leave."

"Sneaking around? Of all the—" Peggy was nearly livid by now.

"I'll take care of this," the man called Alex said. "You'd better go back up to the house."

Allison's glance flickered across Peggy and back to him. She nodded, and started wordlessly past Peggy.

48

Peggy reached out to grab her wrist. "Now wait just a minute," she said, "You listen to me—"

"No, you listen to me." The man's powerful fingers closed over Peggy's hand. She let go of Allison, and without hesitation Allison hurried away in the direction of the house. Peggy found herself held firmly in place, not only by the grip of his hand on hers, but by the icy stare of his eyes.

"This is private property." He spoke slowly but firmly, enunciating each word with exaggerated precision. "We don't take kindly to strangers poking around. Now I would suggest that you get back into your boat and head for the mainland, or Put-in-Bay, or wherever you were headed. And don't come back here."

"It may be private property," Peggy responded heatedly, "but that girl is my sister and I do not intend to leave until I find out what you've done to her to make her behave like that."

"Your what?" He laughed then, but it was not a warm laugh, nor did it do anything to lessen the tension. "I see."

"No, I don't think you do."

"I see that you are either a practical joker, up to some sort of stunt, or you are completely mad. In either case, I must insist again that you leave." He did not wait for her to agree, but holding firmly to her hand, piloted her through the gate, toward the landing where her boat was tied up.

"Where is Mrs. Denver?" Peggy asked. "I know she's here too. I demand to speak to her."

They had reached the landing. He let go her wrist and

stepped back a pace from her. "There is no one here by that name," he said.

"Then tell Allison—"

"Nor by that name either."

"I don't care what name she's using, I want to see her." She moved as if she would go by him and start toward the house again, but he stepped into her path, and his manner was so menacing that for the first time since he had appeared on the scene she felt a twinge of fear.

"My dear young lady," he said, and now his voice was so low that it did indeed sound ominous. "So far we have tried to treat you as nicely as possible under the circumstances. But I can assure you we have treated other trespassers and troublemakers with much less gentleness, and you have made a nuisance of yourself. I will tell you for the last time: Get off this island."

For a moment more Peggy tried to stare him down. But she saw that he was prepared to back up his threats, and fearful of what he might do, she backed down. With a last glance at the imposing lion gates, she clambered down into the boat. He came to untie the lines while she started the engine. His nearness gave her a sense of alarm; she half expected him to change his mind after all and throw her into the drink. Certainly he looked strong enough, and mean enough, to do just that, and she was glad when the boat began to slowly move away from the dock.

He watched her go, standing on the dock with his arms folded across his chest. She had toyed with the idea that perhaps she would only pretend to leave, then circle back when he had gone, but apparently he was not going to give her any such opportunity. He gave no sign of budging until she was well out of sight.

With a sigh of frustration she pushed her hair back from her face and headed the boat toward Ives Point. Her thoughts seethed and churned as violently as the water in her wake.

What on earth had Allison gotten herself into now? That was the crucial question. Why had she pretended she didn't know Peggy, and that she wasn't Allison? What hold did these people, strangers until two days ago, have over her that they could force her to run away with them in the middle of the night, to that strange island house, to pretend that she was not even herself, and deny recognition to the person supposedly closest to her in the world?

That thought brought Peggy up short. But *was* she the closest person to Allison in the world? Apparently not, or Allison would not have denied her just now; unless she was in danger, unless she was afraid to admit the truth. Perhaps she had known that that man was close enough to hear. Perhaps she hadn't dared speak frankly for fear of the consequences. But *what* consequences?

And yet Allison hadn't seemed afraid, she had seemed angry—yet very much at home, very confident of herself, yes, even haughty.

For the first time, Peggy realized that she didn't really know her adopted sister very well at all.

Chapter 7

The sheriff to whom Peggy spoke in town was polite but no more sympathetic than the policeman had been back in Hunter's Point.

"Look, Miss Conners, I'd like to help you, but I don't see exactly what it is you expect of the law. This girl, your sister, you say she's legally of age, you say you talked to her on Lions Island, that she was moving about freely, not as if she were a prisoner or anything like that—which, believe me, knowing the Lions family, would be pretty hard to put stock in anyway. It sounds to me like she's just decided to go there of her own volition and there's not much you or I can do about it."

He folded his hands in his lap and stared at her in a friendly but not very encouraging way.

"But I don't believe she did go there of her own volition," Peggy protested. "And I don't believe she's staying there of her own volition either. I'm sure there's something terribly wrong going on there, something involving my sister, and I mean to find out what it is. If you can't or won't help me I'll find out for myself."

"Miss, the Lionses have been here for generations.

They are very important people to this community, and they enjoy a fine reputation."

"In other words, you're afraid to question them for fear of repercussions? Right by might, is that what you're telling me?"

He met her gaze evenly and there was a glint of anger in his eyes. Finally, after a lengthy pause, he said, "All right, have it your way. I'll go out to Lions Island and see if they can shed any light on things."

"I'll go with you," Peggy said, springing to her feet. For a moment she thought he would veto this suggestion, but finally, with another cold look at her, he nodded, and she followed him from the office.

Lions Island looked no less ominous to her this time, even though she was in the company of the sheriff and two members of the Lake Patrol. The island still seemed to draw in upon itself as they approached. It was evening and the lake mist had begun to hang about the stone wall and the distant roof of the chateau. She thought how total the darkness would be, out here on the water away from city lights and city sounds. Was Allison frightened here at night?

Oh, Allison, Allison, she thought despairingly, what have you gotten yourself into this time?

The boat slowed and in a few moments they were clambering onto the landing. As they did so, Peggy saw a man approaching. She thought at first it was the same man she had met earlier and despite the three strong men with her she felt a twinge of fear. But as she watched him draw nearer she saw she was mistaken; she had never seen this man before. He looked like the other, but thinner; he was handsome, too, in much the same way, but he had a taut, whiplike quality about him, as if he were tensed for some sort of violent action. He wore sunglasses that made it hard to read his expression.

"Evening, Jack," the sheriff greeted him.

"Sheriff, boys." The man nodded and his eyes went from the men to Peggy, but unlike that other man, he gave her a friendly smile. "What can I do for you?"

Peggy started to answer but the sheriff cut her off sharply. "This young lady seems to think you've got her sister a prisoner here."

His eyebrows shot up and he allowed himself a faint chuckle. "Well, one hardly knows what to say. The last time I looked the dungeons were empty. But you're welcome to come have a look, if you like."

"I think I'll have to, Jack. You boys wait here, this won't take long."

"I'll come with you," Peggy said quickly.

"You'll wait here," the sheriff said in a voice that brooked no argument. "You boys see that this young lady doesn't go wandering off anyplace on her own."

She watched them pass through the lion gate and start along the gravel path. She had a sense of renewed frustration; but at least the sheriff would see Allison, and if Allison were simply afraid to admit who she was, she would no longer have cause to be afraid with the lawman right there. Whatever hold these people had on her, once the danger was removed Allison would set it straight. In a few minutes she expected to see them coming along the drive again, Allison alongside the sheriff. She went along the dock and sat beside one of the pilings, leaning back against it, and watched the sun sinking into the distant water.

I'll be glad when this is all over, she thought with a weary sigh.

It was not to be over so quickly, though. When at last she saw the sheriff walking back through the lion gates, he was accompanied not by Allison, but by the same handsome smiling man as before, the one he had addressed as Jack. She scrambled to her feet, brushing off her skirt, and started along the dock to meet them.

"Let's go," the lawman greeted her brusquely. He nodded to the lake patrolmen and they hurried to cast off the boat.

"But I don't understand," Peggy said, looking from the sheriff to Jack. "Where's Allison?"

"That I can't tell you, miss, but I can tell you one thing. She's not here."

"But that can't be! Did you go everywhere, see everything?"

"I saw everything I needed to see. I saw old Jacob Lions, one of the nicest, most generous men this state's ever known, and I felt ashamed of myself, coming up here bothering folks. He's sick, miss, damned sick, that's why they don't want anyone hanging around making a big racket. That's why they didn't want you running all over the place hollering about your sister. They don't want him disturbed, and I don't blame them."

She wilted under the man's barely controlled anger. "I'm sorry," she said meekly. "Truly. But if he's so ill, he might not know she's there. Of course, it wouldn't be his fault."

"It sure isn't. And as for his not knowing, let me tell you, I didn't just talk to him. I talked to Jack here, and his brother, and to their niece. I even talked to old

56

Jacob's financial advisor, and to one of the servants. Now, miss, it's just not conceivable that this sister of yours could be here, on this little island, and none of them know anything about it.''

"But . . .'' She wanted to say, 'they could be lying,' but checked herself. She was aware that she was the center of attention, none of it friendly. The sheriff was angry, the lake patrolmen watching her with amusement. Only Jack Lions seemed sympathetic.

"It's all right, Sheriff,'' he said. "I can understand how the young lady feels. No doubt she's worried about her missing sister, and anxiety sometimes makes us jump to faulty conclusions.''

In the face of his kind voice and sympathetic manner she felt indeed foolish. "I'm sorry to have caused so much trouble,'' she murmured, unable to meet his gentle gaze.

"It's just one of those Leo traits,'' he said with a smile. "Boldness in the cause of right. And I've no doubt you were convinced you were right.''

"I was—but it seems I was mistaken in my conviction.''

"If that's all settled, then let's be shoving off. It's getting dark, and my wife's going to wonder what happened to me,'' the law officer said, jumping down into the boat.

Shamefacedly she followed; Jack Lions came to help her into the boat, squeezing her hand and holding it a fraction of a second longer than was necessary. The patrolmen were quick to cast off, and before she could take a seat in the rear of the boat they were moving away from the dock.

She sat despondently by herself in the back, looking

out over the now dark water and wishing she could clear her mind of her confused and troubled thoughts. She had made a fool of herself. Worse, she had alienated the man she would have to ask to help her find Allison.

But I *have* found Allison, she thought stubbornly. I know where she is—I just don't know why she's there, or why no one will admit she is Allison.

She remembered something then, and moved up in the boat to put a cautious hand on the sheriff's shoulder. He turned his head to glower at her.

"Sheriff, did you see Mrs. Denver?"

"There's no one there by that name either," he said. They were shouting to make themselves heard over the roar of the boat. The town was looming up rapidly ahead of them, the nose of the boat lifting out of the water as it raced for home.

She made her way to the rear again and sat thinking. No Mrs. Denver either. That created another possibility then: that since her first visit Mrs. Denver and Allison, knowing she was sure to be back with the authorities, had left, to avoid exposure. But where would they have gone next?

Or were they even there, she asked herself unhappily. Everyone was so sure she was mistaken; was it possible that in her worry over Allison she had truly made such a mistake?

Suddenly a thought came to her, a memory. Jack Lions, smiling sympathetically and saying, "It's just one of those Leo traits."

But how could he have known that she was a Leo? No one had mentioned that, surely. But Mrs. Denver had known, and Allison. And they must have talked to him about her—discussed their "problem" and how to cope with it.

They were back at the dock and the sheriff was offering his hand to help her out of the boat. She took it and clambered out, but now she stood with her shoulders firmly back, her chin up once more. Now suddenly she knew that she had not been mistaken, that Allison was there, or had been there, Allison and Mrs. Denver. Unwittingly Jack had given her the confirmation she needed, the evidence to prove, to herself at least, that she was right and the lawman wrong. She knew that she would never convince him of that, not without further evidence, but in her own mind there was complete certainty.

"Well, sorry I couldn't help you, miss," the lawman was saying. "I'd advise you to go back home and wait till you hear from your sister. It's my bet she'll show up."

"Yes, I'm sure she will," Peggy said. "Good night, Sheriff." She left him there and walked back toward the streets of the town—not to head for home, as he had suggested, but to look for a hotel. She was equally sure that Allison would show up—right here, in town. And she intended to be here when she did.

Chapter 8

"Coffee, miss?"

Peggy started and glanced up at the young waitress beside her. She had been far away, in a gloomy landscape of her own fears and concerns, most of them centered on Allison.

"Please," Peggy said, managing a wan smile. She felt pale and drawn this morning, after a nearly sleepless night. For one thing, she'd had to call home once she had checked into this motel, and tell her parents of Allison's mysterious disappearance and her subsequent strange behavior.

"But I don't understand," her mother had said. "If you've found Allison, isn't that the end of it? Let me talk to her, can you, I'll straighten her out in a hurry."

Peggy had to explain patiently that Allison was not with her, and again that Allison insisted that she was not Allison.

"I think you'd better come home," was her father's advice. "Leave this business up to the authorities."

"But the authorities aren't doing anything. They keep telling me that Allison left of her own will, and there's nothing they can do."

"Then there's nothing you can do either."

At length she had persuaded them to her view; she would stay where she was for a few days, just until she had an opportunity to see Allison alone and get the truth out of her.

"Then I'll come home, with or without her," Peggy had promised, and ended the conversation before they had an opportunity to insist otherwise.

Afterward, though, in the darkness of the night, she had had to face the problem more squarely. She did not know how she was going to manage to see Allison again, especially alone. The stone beasts at the lion-gate guarded her as effectively as if they were real animals. Behind them was Allison, and the answers to all the maddening questions she had raised; but how to reach her?

"You must be the girl who's looking for her sister," the waitress said, putting Peggy's breakfast in front of her.

Again, Peggy was startled from her reverie. She nearly knocked her orange juice over. "I beg your pardon," she said.

The waitress looked embarrassed. "Gee, sorry, I didn't mean to butt in—the sheriff is my uncle, and he was over for a barbecue last night, so we got the whole story. It's a drag, isn't it?"

"I'll say," Peggy murmured and then, more interestedly, "Do you know the Lions family?"

"Me?" She looked astonished at the suggestion. "Gosh, hardly, they're not in my class, if you know what I mean."

"But you do know of them?"

The waitress glanced over her shoulder. Only one

other table in the coffee shop was occupied, and it was being tended by the other waitress. "Oh, sure, I know who they are and stuff like that. But they don't exactly mingle here in town, they stick to themselves—I guess you noticed that."

"I got that impression. How many of them are there, by the way?"

"Mmm, well, old Jacob Lions, of course, he was head of the clan, so to speak, although I hear he's pretty sick these days. His wife died years ago but she was nice, as I remember, friendlier than the rest of them, at least to me. Of course I was just a little girl."

"He has only the two sons?" Peggy suggested, eager to bring the girl back to the present.

"Just one, Alex. Jack is kind of a cousin or something. No one knows much about him. He doesn't come into town very often. When he does, he has an eye for the girls, I think."

"And Alex is stand-offish?"

The girl shrugged and again glanced around the shop. "Actually, he hasn't been around here much either. He was living in France—the family has some wine properties there too, I hear. He just came home a few days ago."

"And there's a girl there too, right?"

"That's Melissa, old Jacob's granddaughter. She just came back too."

Peggy started to ask something more but the girl said, "Excuse me," and went off to take care of a couple who had just come in.

Waiting impatiently for the waitress to finish with her customers, Peggy felt the first stirrings of hope since she had gotten up that morning. A granddaughter who had been away and recently returned. Allison, just arriving here. Somehow, she thought, that may be the missing link in the chain: Some sort of link between Melissa and Allison.

It was ten minutes before the waitress returned to her table, bearing a coffeepot. She refilled Peggy's cup and would have gone on with her work but Peggy stopped her with another question.

"This granddaughter, Melissa, has she been living in France too?"

"No, it's kind of far out, really. She was dead. I mean, everyone thought she'd been dead for years. Her and her mother died in a boat accident, only they never found Melissa's body; she was a little girl then. But everyone thought she was dead, everyone except old Jacob Lions. I guess he always believed she was just missing, and from what I hear, he's spent a fortune all these years trying to find her. I guess he made himself believe someone had found her and adopted her, if you know what I mean. And then, just a few days ago, there was a rumor going around town that they'd finally found her.

Peggy tried not to sound too pleased by this bit of news. "How?" she asked. "How did they find her?"

The girl shrugged. "The detectives, I guess. I heard he had a whole force of private detectives looking for her all these years—it's been fifteen years or so, I don't know exactly how long, but I was just a little kid, you know."

"Yes, I see," Peggy said and nodded. She could not suppress a feeling of triumph. The return of the missing granddaughter, and Allison's strange behavior, were just too much to be coincidence.

"Look, I've got to get back to work, people are starting to come in," the waitress said.

"Thanks for all the help," Peggy said. "I'm Peggy Conners, by the way."

"My name's Sally—excuse me." She hurried to where a family group was waiting to order breakfast.

Peggy, who had done little more then pick at her food, found herself too excited now to think of eating. She collected her purse, paid the check, and left.

Outside, though, her triumph faded a little in the bright morning sunlight. What she had learned only furthered her suspicions, but she had no more in the way of evidence that she could present to the authorities. If she was going to change the sheriff's mind and persuade him to help her she needed something concrete, something that he couldn't dismiss with a scowl and a shrug. She stood by her car, head down, pondering this dilemma. When she looked up, she saw Allison.

Allison was in the Rolls, and driving it was not Waldo but Jack Lions. They were headed south, out of town.

Without a moment's hesitation Peggy was in her car, the Jaguar's engine roaring to life. She darted out into traffic, almost taking the fender off an approaching Buick, earning herself a honk of the horn and a few choice words from the angry driver, but she had no time now to pause and apologize to him. She cut in and out of the morning traffic, pursuing the Rolls.

Just when she thought she had lost them, she caught a glimpse of silver gray ahead and in a moment more she was in sight of the car. She slowed down, hanging back so that, with luck, they would not notice her if they happened to glance back. She wasn't sure, exactly what she would do—she had a vague idea that if she stayed with them as far as they were going, she might have an opportunity to talk to Allison alone.

"Of course, for all I know," she thought grimly as she changed lanes to pass a slow-moving car, "they may be on their way to Florida."

They left the town and the car ahead began to gain speed. That didn't worry Peggy; old and battered-looking though her car was, she knew it was an easy match for the luxurious sedan ahead. Nor was she the least bit afraid of driving fast. She was a good driver, and knew it.

Ahead of her, taillights flickered red; they were slowing down, then turning into a gas station. She bit her lip anxiously. She couldn't just pull in behind them without being noticed, and there was no place to pull off the road between here and there. The only thing she could do was go on by, and hope no one saw or recognized her.

She passed another car, keeping it between her and the gas station, where the Rolls was now parked at the pumps. She didn't dare risk looking over to see if they had noticed her.

Once past the station, she changed to the right lane, slowing down, and when she approached a side road, she turned into it and waited, looking back the way she had come for the Rolls to come into view again.

The time dragged by. She glanced at her watch impatiently. Three minutes, four . . . surely it shouldn't take any longer than that to fill a gas tank. Could they have seen her, and turned back to lose her?

Should she start back—and risk passing them going the wrong way?

She waited another three minutes. By then it was obvious that something had gone wrong. It took her a moment more to back onto the busy highway. Slamming the car angrily into gear, she raced back the way she had just come.

There was no sign of them at the gas station, nor anywhere along the road. She slowed down as she drove into the town again, angry and frustrated. They had eluded her after all, obviously turning back while she waited stupidly for them to pass her. There was a ferry that cut from the point back to the mainland; no doubt they had left the highway and come back to that. But when she drove to the landing she saw the ferry in the distance, already on its way; there was no way she could find out if they were on it, and no point in further pursuit.

Despondently, she went back to her motel. She still had no plans; she was here, and meant to stay until she had at least talked to Allison. But to do that it looked as if she would have to return to the island; and how was she to do that without just being thrown off again, perhaps bodily this time? Tired, and shaken, she stepped to her door and turned the key.

At first, as she stepped into the relative darkness of her room, she thought the maid was in the process of cleaning it. Then, as she realized the truth, she gasped and stepped back in surprise and disbelief.

Someone had ransacked her room. Her case lay open on the floor, its contents strewn about. The drawers of the dresser and the nightstand had been yanked out violently, left open or, in one case, thrown on the floor. The bed itself had been searched, the mattress lying askew as if someone had yanked it up to look under it, and the bedclothes flung about.

It was the same throughout the room, and the bathroom, where she had left her cosmetics case. Jars of cold cream had been opened, her perfume bottle was lying empty in the sink, its contents apparently down the drain.

She stared at the disorder, and before her dismay could overwhelm her, she felt the sharp, primitive pangs of instinctual fear. Who could have done this, and why? What could they possibly have been looking for?

Chapter 9

The manager of the motel was very apologetic. "We've never had anything like this happen before," he insisted. "I don't understand it."

The police—not the sheriff but the local police—had been called at once. Peggy volunteered none of her own suspicions this time. Without some evidence, something concrete that she could show, she felt this stern-looking officer would be no more likely to believe her story about the Lionses than the sheriff had been.

And at any rate, there was no tangible evidence that the Lionses had done this. On the surface, this was a burglary, pure and simple. A check had revealed that several things were missing. She had left some cash in her case, and it was gone, along with the transistor radio she had carried there, and a portable television belonging to the motel. But the missing articles did not convince Peggy that this was a simple burglary. If someone from Lions Island had searched her room, for whatever reason, they would have to cover their tracks; they may well have taken these things to throw suspicion away from them.

"But why only one room?" the manager asked.

"Hard to say," the policeman answered. "These people don't always make sense. Maybe something scared them off before they worked the other rooms, or they thought Miss Connors, here, looked more likely to have something of value. A lot of crime today, it's just kids, poor scared kids. No telling what goes through their minds, either."

The manager nodded. Then, turning to Peggy, "If you'd like another room," he suggested tentatively.

"No, that won't be necessary, if you can just have this cleaned up." Whoever had found her in this room would certainly be able to find her in another if they planned a second visit. There was little point, she thought, in moving to a fresh one. Whoever had been here was determined to find whatever they were looking for.

But what had they been looking for? Again the question pushed at her thoughts when the policeman and the motel manager had finally left her alone, while she was refolding her scattered clothes. Something to tie her to Allison? Perhaps some evidence of Allison's real identity?

For the first time she realized that if the Lions family, and Allison, were engaged in something illegal—and she couldn't begin to think what it might be—then she was a genuine threat to them, because she was the one person who knew who Allison was—and might eventually find some way of proving it.

Another thought occurred to her: Was it possible that Jack Lions and Allison, having seen her following them and eluded her, had come back here to search her room? Surely they hadn't known where she was staying, but it was a small town. By now local people knew who she was, and it wouldn't have taken more than a few minutes for Jack Lions to ask the right question of the right people to find her.

She was playing a dangerous game, that much was clear, and with formidable opponents, people who were used to having their own way, people with enough money and power to back up that kind of arrogance.

In the end, there was only one thing that she could do, must do; she must go back to Lions Island, without the sheriff or the lake patrol. She must find Allison, alone, and talk to her. After that, if Allison still insisted on staying, on doing whatever it was she had set out to do, then Peggy was willing to wash her hands of the entire business. But first, she must see Allison.

And that meant another journey to Lions Island, to the great stone lions at the gate.

As if her intention had sent out some sort of signal, she was visited by the sheriff. She was surprised to find him at her door, and a little wary too. His expression on seeing her was not exactly a friendly or an encouraging one.

"Miss Conners," he greeted her brusquely, nodding. "I see you're still around."

"Yes," was all she said. He waited for more, some explanation, some excuse; when he saw that it wasn't forthcoming, he changed his hat from one hand to another.

"How long were you planning on staying, miss?"

"I'm not sure exactly. A day or two perhaps. Why, sheriff?"

"Miss Conners, there are laws against harassing people, and making a pest of yourself at their expense.

I'd hate to have to lock you up, just to get you off the Lionses' backs.''

''Is that a threat, Sheriff?'' Their eyes met in combat; but he was not so brazen as to allow that statement to stand.

''No, just a simple statement of fact. You start harrassing those people, and I will enforce the law.'' Then, his tone softening, he said, ''Look, miss, why don't you take my advice and go home and wait. Leave finding your sister up to the authorities.''

''The authorities? People like you, you mean? How much effo t have you expended in trying to help me, or my sister? You won't even listen to what I've been trying to tell you. What kind of faith can you expect me to have in the authorities?'' She emphasized this last word with angry sarcasm.

He had the good grace to look embarrassed. Lamely, he said, ''We aren't talking about a runaway child, Miss Conners, we're talking about an adult. Wherever she is, whatever she's doing, it's really up to her.''

''Is it? I want to find that out for myself.''

''Well, you've been warned, that's all.'' With that he left her, slamming his cap angrily back on his head. This effrontery both angered and dismayed her; she felt even more isolated than before, more removed from any real help. She knew now that she could only act alone—and in the face of official disapproval.

At the dock, she made arrangements for a boat later that evening; she had decided it would be easier to approach the island unnoticed if she went at night. She had no exact plans for what she would do once she arrived there. She would trust to luck that something would happen to show her the way.

Of course, there was the possibility that Allison was no longer on the island; when she had seen her and Jack Lions in the car this morning, they might have been on their way to a new hideaway, some place where Allison would be removed from any danger of discovery.

An idea had come to her, though; she knew that on the mainland they drove a Rolls-Royce, but she also knew that the boat she had seen Waldo piloting to the island was certainly not big enough to transport a car. That meant that the car must be kept somewhere on the mainland, presumably somewhere near where their boat was kept.

It was not hard to find. Old George, from whom she had rented the boat, pointed out a sidestreet leading away from the docks, where there were a number of garages. Number twelve, he informed her, belonged to the Lionses.

"But I wouldn't go messing around there, if I were you," he added.

"Oh, of course not, I was just curious," she assured him. But he had no sooner turned his attention to a new customer, a heavy-set man in a bright flowered shirt and Bermuda shorts, than she had strolled in the direction of the garages.

The door to number twelve was locked, but there was enough of an opening for her to see a glint of silver gray within. The Rolls was back; that might or might not mean that Allison was back on the island—there was really only one way for her to know for sure.

Chapter 10

Her one fear had been that in the darkness she might have difficulty locating the island, but she had set her course in what she knew to be the general direction, and as she had left behind the lights of the town she had soon been able to distinguish the soft glow of the lights of Lions Island. There were floodlights at the boat landing, and further inland the lights of the house cast their own gleam. They turned the smooth surface of the water to a hammered bronze.

She skirted the island, avoiding the brightly lighted landing. Surely those gates could not be the only way through the wall. There must be another exit as well, for safety's sake, and perhaps another landing.

She circled nearly all the way around the island, cutting her engine back almost to an idle, and staying well out from the beach. She was disappointed in not finding another dock, but on the northern side the beach looked sandy and smooth. When she saw that she was again coming around to the lighted area of the boat-house and the gates, she swung back and made her way to the far side of the island. She brought the boat in slowly, as quietly as possible, and beached it. She had sighted a cluster of rocks, and she waded in to tie the boat up to these. She tied it carefully; the last thing she wanted was to be stranded here.

Once actually on the island she stood indecisively for a moment. She was outside the wall and, as nearly as she had been able to judge coming in, at the rear of the house, beyond the other, utilitarian buildings that she took to be wine presses and the like. Before her loomed the stone wall, high enough to completely block her view. She supposed a real trespasser would have been able to scale it, but it looked to her an impossible task.

She had brought a flashlight, and had dressed in jeans and sneakers, unsure of just what she might have to do to gain entrance. For now, though, it seemed most sensible just to walk. She clung to her idea that there must be another gate in the wall encircling the island, and so she set off, following the wall, to try to find it.

She was soon glad she had dressed sensibly. Much of her ''walk'' was over difficult, rocky terrain. The wall in places came right down to the water's edge, and she found herself wading in water that once or twice came up to her knees. She scraped her hands and legs, and got what she was sure would be an ugly bruise on one shin. And when finally the wall veered away from the water and the rocks, it was replaced by clumps of thick bushes. Pushing through them, she kept her spirits up by contemplating exactly what she was going to say to Allison when she found her.

''If I find her,'' she amended glumly.

Finally, just when she was about to give up all hope, she came around a curve in the wall and found herself almost directly in front of a little wooden door. And now, looking out toward the lake, she could see the remains of what had once been another landing. This at one time must have been the back entrance, although it looked as if it had been many years since it had been used.

She pushed against the old door, holding her breath. At first she thought it was locked; it didn't budge. But she pushed again and slowly, laboriously, it creaked inward, on rusted hinges. The noise it made sounded to her frightened ears like the scream of a banshee, and for a moment she stood frozen in place, listening to the pounding of her heart. Within, everything remained silent and still.

Finally, her skin tingling with excitement, she stepped through the opening.

She was at the edge of a vineyard. A stone walk, crumbling and overgrown with grass, led along the wall, presumably up to the rear of the house. Off to her right, in the distance, she could see the dark outlines of the winery and of the house itself.

Now that she was actually inside the wall, she was faced with the real question, the one she had avoided trying to answer in advance—how was she to find Allison?

"The last time, Allison found me," she thought. "She was out strolling. Maybe she will be again."

She began to steal along the path, staying close to the old wall, as much out of the light as possible. Fortunately, the moon had not risen, and the house lights cast no more than a faint glow here.

She reached a huge, barnlike building, and crossed the path to pause in its shadows. Not far ahead a rectangle of light spilled from a window and she thought she saw a shadow flicker across it. Perhaps this was where a watchman lived, or even the chauffeur, Waldo. The building seemed to go on forever in the other direction. She would have to creep all the way around it, or manage to get past the lighted window unnoticed.

If only she had been able to see more of the island in the daylight, see beyond the walls and get a lay of the land. No doubt there were lawns and gardens about the house, and if Allison were out strolling, that would be the logical place to. find her. But whether the lawns were in front of, or behind, or to the side of the house, she couldn't guess.

She took a deep breath and moved forward; when she got to the lighted window, she would simply have to crawl on her hands and knees past it, and hope that no one chose that moment to idly glance out.

Faintly, in the distance, she heard the sound of music. Someone was playing a piano, or perhaps it was a record. Chopin. The crisp notes seemed to drift and echo on the evening breeze along with the bittersweet scent of the grapevines. What an incongruous accompaniment it made to the frightened beating of her heart as she sensed a vague danger, a presence . . .

And suddenly the music, the grape scent, everything, was gone, everything but her fear, and the feel of a pair of hands seizing her roughly, jerking her about.

Her heart thudding, she stared up into the angry, handsome face of Alex Lions.

"What are you doing here?" he demanded.

She, who had felt so daring, so courageous, bleated in a voice like a frightened lamb, "I had to try to see her," before her voice failed her altogether. She stood quaking in his grip, staring wide-eyed at him.

When he suddenly released her, she was so weak-kneed she nearly sank to the ground. For support, she leaned back against the solid concrete of the building behind her. She knew she was trembling, knew he was aware of her fear. Perhaps that was why when he spoke again it was less viciously.

"You're still sticking to that story?"

"Because it's the truth." Somehow she managed to find the voice to insist on that.

He looked angered again for a moment. Then, with a gesture that might have been impatience, frustration—she wasn't sure what—he grabbed her again, less gently than before, and steered her toward a door into the concrete building. She was too disconcerted to resist, though for all she knew he might have been going to fling her down a well. Although, on second thought, she didn't think so. There was something about him, something not exactly kind, nor even pleasant, but something decent—a lack of malice.

He took her inside. It was dark and she could see nothing but a narrow beam of light that came from a slightly opened door. He led her toward it. Once inside, she could see nothing, the light blinding her after all her time in the darkness. But gradually, blinking and squinting against it, she saw that they were in an office, not a carpeted and paneled office like her father's, but a crude, working man's office, with a battered desk, the most ancient adding machine she had ever seen, papers and books piled everywhere. It was cluttered and dusty, but it looked used, and functional.

She saw too, now that she could look at him less hysterically, that Alex Lions did not appear the wealthy scion of the family but more like one of his own workmen. He wore faded and dirty jeans, an old shirt open to the waist, thick-soled leather boots. Of a sudden, she liked him for that; she realized that he had been out here working, rather than lounging inside somewhere lazily sipping a brandy. She saw at the same time that he was used to working. The hands that had gripped her so powerfully were a working man's hands, callused and hard-looking, right now even a little dirty. And his face, his neck, the chest she saw exposed by the open shirt, had the near burnt brown color that is only acquired in days, weeks, months, out in the sun—a farmer's skin. A grape picker's skin.

He did not, of course, stand politely and wait for her to study him. As they came in, he went to one of the chairs and began to toss papers and books from it onto the floor. When it was emptied, he even yanked a handkerchief from his pocket and wiped it clean—for me, she thought, and nearly giggled at the absurdity of such a chivalrous action being extended to her dirty, ragged, and soggy person. But when he banged the chair over in front of her, she sat meekly in it.

He had not yet spoken since the encounter outside, but now he studied her with a hard, critical gaze. His eyes went from her face—she managed a watery smile which he seemed not to notice—moved down her body, and came back to her face. She wished she didn't look quite so bedraggled.

He took a pack of cigarettes from his pocket, offering her one, which she declined, and lit one for himself.

"Now," he said, exhaling smoke, "Start at the beginning and tell me again, calmly this time, what this is all about."

And that was just what she did. She began with Allison's bad temper because she hadn't had her way about summer vacation, she went on to their trip to Hunter's Point, to that oddly fortuitous meeting with Mrs. Denver—that was the only point at which he interrupted her.

"Mrs. Denver, that was her name?"

"Yes. Do you know her?"

"There's no one around here by that name."

She felt bold enough to push the question: "But you know someone who fits the description. There is someone here on this island like that, isn't there?"

"There's a Mrs. Marvel who lives here."

"Who is she?"

"She is my father's . . ." he hesitated, as if he found it distasteful to admit, "His astrological advisor."

She jumped up from her chair. "Oh, she must be the same, don't you see, Mrs. Denver knew everything about astrology. I knew they must be the same."

"Go on with your story," he said, grinding his cigarette out in an already overflowing ashtray.

She continued her narrative, speaking more confidently now. She sensed that his attitude had changed, not that he exactly believed her, not yet, but that he was no longer adamant in his disbelief. And he was listening, listening quietly, carefully, to everything she had to say.

"And you believe the girl you met down by the gates is your sister?" he said when she had finished.

"I don't merely 'believe' it, I *know* it. I've known Allison all my life, I couldn't be mistaken."

He ran one hand through his hair, ruffling it even

more than before. "And I know she is Melissa Lions—Gilbert, actually, that was her father's name. She's my sister's daughter."

"But how can you be so sure, if she's been missing all these years—" He shot her a surprised glance and she added hastily, "I've talked to people about you, about the family. I found out that Melissa's been gone since she was a little girl, you couldn't have seen her in all that time, or talked to her. How can you know she's Melissa?"

He made an exasperated gesture. "Do you think we are total fools out here on this island?" he demanded impatiently. "Do you think if someone came strolling into the house and said 'I am Melissa, your long lost niece, and incidentally heiress to the Lions fortune' I would just accept that blindly? I've talked to the girl, at length, I've questioned her like a prosecuting attorney. She knows too much, things that only Melissa could possibly know, not things she could have gotten out of newspapers, or even with any amount of ferreting out. Things no one but Melissa could know."

"She could have been coached," Peggy suggested. "Allison is very bright, she has a wonderful memory. Mrs. Denver—or Mrs. Marvel, whichever, could have told her all those details . . ."

"Mrs. Marvel didn't live here then, at that time no one here had ever heard of her."

She said, less hopefully, "Waldo?"

He shook his head. "Not here either. Tell me, where did you say you lived, you and your sister?"

"Columbus."

"According to Mrs. Marvel, Melissa was found in a girls' school in Connecticut. I've questioned her about that area too, and she knows it, too well to have just been coached on that also.''

It was Peggy's turn to sound a trifle smug. ''Allison was going to a girls' school in Connecticut,'' she said simply.

That got through to him finally. His eyebrows lifted slightly and he studied her, as if he thought she might be making that up, and then clearly decided she was not. He lit another cigarette, not bothering to offer her one this time, and went to stand at the window—the lighted window she had seen outside; she realized now that he had done this before, come like this to stand looking out the window, puzzling over something—perhaps this same problem. He seemed for a long time to have forgotten that she was there, and she did not remind him or try to intrude upon his thoughts. She waited, no longer at all afraid of him.

Finally, he said, ''My father is ill, very ill, he doesn't have long to live. I can't have you poking around here, climbing in windows and crawling under beds . . .''

She started to protest but he silenced her with a look. ''I'll give you a chance to prove your story,'' he said. ''But not here, not like this. I'll bring Melissa to you. You can confront her yourself, say what you like. If she is your sister, and I'm not saying for a moment I accept that, it shouldn't be hard to get straight between you.''

''When. . . ?''

''When I can,'' he said, a bit curtly. ''I don't imagine Melissa will exactly be pleased. No, don't start looking stubborn again, I'll bring her to you, to your motel. Now, I think it's time you returned to town and left me to my work. I've got a great deal I want to do, and you've taken up far too much of my time.''

She did not object, nor press him further for a commitment; she sensed that he would do as he had promised, and she let him lead her from the building and back along the walk, the walk she had crept along so stealthily a short time before.

"I'd forgotten this old walkway was here," he said when they got to the door, still standing open.

"I'm glad you forgot it," she said.

Luckily her boat was still there; the tide had come in, and they had to splash through quite a bit of water to get to it. He came along with her, although she insisted it was not necessary. Was he just trying to be helpful—or was his intention to make sure she really left? Peggy couldn't say.

At last, soaked, she was back in the boat. He waited alongside, standing in water that came almost to his waist, until she had gotten the engine started.

"I'll cast off for you," he said.

"Thank you. And thank you for—for listening, at least."

He said nothing to that. Their eyes met once again, but in the darkness she could not read the expression in his. Then he turned and made his way laboriously through the water to the rocks where she had tied up the lines. He cast them off for her and stood waiting, watching, as she began to move away. When she looked back, he was still there, gradually fading into the shadows. She could not tell finally if he was there or not, or when he might have turned back to the house.

She felt less frightened, less desolate now. Certainly less alone. She could not yet consider Alex Lions an ally (indeed, he had told her plainly that he thought Allison was his missing niece), but she felt strangely confident that at least he would give her a fair hearing. He had listened dutifully to what she had had to say, neither arguing nor dismissing; and he had promised to bring Allison to her, so that they could talk things out.

Strangely, though, as she headed the boat back toward town, it was not seeing Allison that she was looking forward to. It was seeing Alex Lions.

Chapter 11

It was late when she arrived back at the town's dock. Old George had already gone for the day, but she had anticipated this and had made arrangements accordingly. She tied up the boat, leaving the key under the seat as arranged, and covered it with the tarp from the back.

The streets were quiet. Although this was a resort area it was a family resort, with few of the late night crowds common to more swinging places. At just eleven, the town exuded tranquility; the sidewalks, as Allison would have put it, were rolled up.

Peggy herself rather enjoyed that. She had none of the fear she might have experienced walking alone at night on the streets of most big cities. If the good people of the town were abed, so apparently, were the bad people.

Thinking of bad people, she was immediately reminded that someone had ransacked her motel room. And Allison and the Lions family, or some part of the household, were certainly involved in something less than legitimate. Even this vacation community had its criminal element, and she would be wise to remember that, to not let down her guard, to keep her wits honed—if she was ever to solve this mystery.

Alex's comments earlier had made her realize for the first time that Allison was not just pretending that she was not Allison, she was pretending to be a rich heiress, granddaughter to a wealthy old man who was ill, perhaps at death's door. Allison—who had always been spoiled, pampered, who had always felt she was not getting her fair share, who always wanted more, who craved not just money but all the accoutrements of wealth.

It was true, for all their years together, for all their vaunted closeness, she had never really known Allison at all. The girl she had called her sister, the one with whom she had shared all the adventures and thrills, the pleasures and agonies, of growing up, was in fact a stranger to her.

Perhaps, she thought wryly, we are all strangers to one another, going through the motions, pretending to know, to understand, to communicate, while all the time we stand behind glass walls.

She reached the motel. Its rows of windows were dark, the other guests already abed. Her heels echoed hollowly as she walked along the row of locked doors. At her own, she hesitated. Perhaps her strange thoughts, the events of the past few days, or just plain tiredness were playing havoc with her nerves, but suddenly she was afraid to go in. She sensed something, an alien presence. For a full moment she stood with her hand on the doorknob.

"What nonsense," she told herself, and went in. It was dark and she could not remember where the light was; on the nightstand, surely. But hadn't she left a light on?

As if to prove to herself that she was not afraid, that she was being silly, she resisted her impulse to leave the door open for light. She closed it, and the room went black, as black as a tomb.

She took a step toward the nightstand—and froze, recognizing the scent of tobacco smoke. She turned toward the two chairs that sat by the window, and saw the glow of red, the tip of someone's cigarette. Faintly, barely discernible, was the shadow of someone seated in the chair, framed against the pale light at the window.

She found the light switch, the one by the door that she had forgotten. It clicked, and the lights, soft, unobtrusive, came on.

Mrs. Denver smiled, a trifle acidly, from the striped Danish chair, her cigarette frozen midway in its arc to her lips. Behind the veil of her hat, she blinked once or twice, owlishly. She looked younger than Peggy remembered her. Younger and more menacing.

"I made myself at home," Mrs. Denver said. "I knew you would want me to be comfortable while I waited."

"In the dark?"

"This light is so—so unflattering. A young girl never thinks of that. But a woman of my years . . ."

She puffed at the cigarette, aggressively, intently. At the same time her hard, shrewd eyes observed Peggy through the cloud of smoke forming about her head.

Peggy, whose room it was and who ought to have

been in command of the situation, was disconcerted. She felt as if she were the intruder here, as if she were somehow in the wrong. Defensively, a bit shrilly, she asked, "What do you want?"

"Why did you come here?"

The question caught her off guard. She crossed the room self-consciously and dropped her purse and sweater on the bed.

"I came to find Allison, as you well know," she said, turning back. She was disturbed, but also a little angry at being attacked like this.

"Your sister is not here." The cigarette glowed, faded, glowed. The veiled woman smoked rapidly, tensely.

"That's a lie and you know it," Peggy shot back. "She's on Lions Island. I've seen her and talked to her. You must be mad, both of you, to think that I would see you, meet you, talk to you, and not know who you are, that I would be talked into believing she is not Allison, that you are not Mrs. Denver, whatever name you use. Of course, I suppose you never thought I would find you here, did you?"

"That's true. I thought you were a bit of a namby-pamby—not typical Leo, mind you, but then Leos generally don't like to go to a lot of trouble. I thought once you'd made your inquiries you'd go haughtily back to Cincinnati . . ."

"Columbus," Peggy corrected her instinctively.

". . . and wait, which is exactly what you should have done. Nothing here is any of your business."

"You involve my sister in some sort of silly scheme, steal her away in the middle of the night, and expect me to regard it as none of my business?'' Peggy was incredulous.

Mrs. Denver ground her cigarette in the ashtray. It lay smoldering beside numerous others; she had apparently waited some time for Peggy to return.

"Not your sister, your adopted sister—no blood relation at all, really. She couldn't be, because she is Melissa Gilbert, the child that Jacob Lions lost years ago, the child I have been searching for, that I found for him, that only I could have found for him, because I knew better than to use his silly detectives, I used the one infallible source of information—the stars.''

"And they guided you to my sister?'' Peggy said derisively.

"It might interest you to know that I did *not* steal her away. I presented her with the truth, with the facts, and she came freely, of her own will.''

"Like a thief in the night.''

"She knew that you would never understand, that you would only be a hindrance, a nuisance, as she put it.''

Mrs. Denver withdrew a cigarette case from her purse.

Watching her, Peggy was stung by the remark, foolishly so, because she knew that it had been intended to sting, to throw her off. And yet she could imagine, faintly imagine, Allison saying just such a thing, and it hurt, after all her worrying, after all her care, all her efforts, it hurt to think that Allison might have described her as a nuisance. She was silent for a long moment.

"So you see," Mrs. Denver concluded smugly,

once again puffing earnestly on a cigarette, "it really is none of your business."

Peggy turned angrily away, knowing that she was being manipulated by this shrewd, heartless woman. Suddenly she saw, in a flash of insight, how much more easily Allison must have been handled. Poor, foolish Allison, with all her grandiose dreams, with her greedy ambition, it was easy to play on her ego, on her self-centeredness. This woman must have seen all that at once; Allison would have been putty in her hands.

"I will accept that," she said firmly, "when Allison tells me so herself."

"You will never hear it from her because you will never have the opportunity to talk to her."

Her anger lowering her guard, Peggy nearly turned and said, "I have already arranged to talk to her." But even as she turned she checked herself. Instinct told her that Mrs. Denver might stop at nothing to thwart that meeting; Peggy was well aware that this was a woman of strong mind and will—a dangerous woman. Allison would never be able to stand up to her.

"We shall see," was all Peggy allowed herself to say.

Her confidence, which she could not entirely disguise, penetrated Mrs. Denver's smug arrogance. She seemed suddenly angry and her cigarette joined the others in the ashtray.

"I am not asking you, I am telling you. Give this up. Leave here. Go home. If Allison chooses to contact you in the future, she will do so, without any prodding or snooping from you. You have my word on that."

This time Peggy did turn back to face her. "I don't

like being told what to do," she said slowly, evenly. "You say that I have no claim on Allison. I deny it is so, I will not say it is so until I have spoken personally, and alone, with Allison. But far less do you have a claim on me. I did not invite you here, I do not know how you got in—how did you by the way?"

Mrs. Denver only smiled. It was an ugly smile that did nothing to relieve the tension in the room.

"Well, however you managed it, you can now leave," Peggy said icily. "And you can remember not to come back. I'm here to find Allison, to see Allison. What you do neither concerns me nor interests me. In fact, we have nothing further to say to each other."

Mrs. Denver got up from the chair. For the first time Peggy realized what a big woman she was. She seemed willowy, frail even. She habitually sat with her shoulders slumped, leaning forward, and her movements with her hands were so graceful that, combined with the soft elegance of her gray hair and her expensive, flowing dresses, they created an impression of gentle femininity. But suddenly Peggy realized that Mrs. Denver was tall, wiry, an imposing figure of a woman who had used great skill and taste to overcome a certain mannishness in appearance. Her femininity, her fragility, were illusions, deliberately created. At the moment the illusion was shattered the woman was revealed for what she was: powerful, and dangerous.

"I will warn you once more to leave here. You are meddling in things you don't understand, things that are none of your business. You may get hurt, and you will have only yourself to blame."

Mrs. Denver took several steps toward her. Instinctively Peggy stepped backward, until the edge of the bed bumped against the backs of her legs. She felt cornered, threatened.

"You can't come here and threaten me," she said, annoyed to hear that her voice was tremulous. "The police . . ."

Mrs. Denver laughed a harsh, sinister sound. "The police? Have you forgotten, I am from Lions Island. No one here bothers us. They dare not."

Peggy wanted to deny that statement, but without genuine conviction, the words died in her throat. The authorities here obviously were in awe of the influential Lions clan. She was not entirely certain how far they would go in opposition to them.

Suddenly she was afraid to be in this room, alone, in the middle of the night, with this woman. "Please leave," she said again. "If you don't go at once I'll ring the desk and tell them you broke in here."

"The Lions family owns this motel," Mrs. Denver informed her smugly.

Peggy sank down on the edge of the bed, at a loss for words. Of course it might be a lie, told to undermine her fading confidence. But it might also be true. That would explain how her room had been ransacked, and the ease with which Mrs. Denver had entered her room to wait for her.

For all she knew, the Lions family owned most of the town.

Mrs. Denver came to stand before her, so that Peggy had to lean far back to look into the woman's face.

"For the last time, you are not wanted here. You are not even safe here. Do you understand that? I will tolerate no more interference from you. I have worked

94

too many years, long and hard to . . . to accomplish something. Now I am within reach of my goal. I will not have you, or anyone else, destroy everything I have worked for. You will be gone from here tomorrow—or you will answer for the consequences.''

For a fleeting moment Peggy actually thought Mrs. Denver meant to strike her. Then, abruptly, she turned and stalked across the room. The door opened, closed, and she was gone.

Chapter 12

She was awakened by the ringing of the phone. For a sleepy moment she forgot where she was and lay, half asleep, half awake, waiting for her mother to answer it. Then suddenly she remembered and, sitting up in bed, reached for the phone on the nightstand. It was the desk clerk.

"We have your bill ready for you, Miss Conners," she heard him through her lingering sleepiness.

"My bill? I'm afraid I don't understand."

"But I thought . . . Aren't you leaving this morning?"

"No. Where did you get that idea?" As if, she thought grimly, she didn't know.

"Why, I understood . . ." He hesitated, then said, "I see. Perhaps I'd better look into this further."

"You do that," she said drily.

So, Mrs. Denver hadn't been bluffing, the family did own this motel; and how much more of the town? She got wearily out of bed.

She was not really surprised when the clerk called back while she was brushing her teeth.

"I'm afraid there's been a mix-up," he explained,

speaking smoothly now, too smoothly. "It was my understanding you were only here through last night."

"My stay is indefinite."

"Yes, of course. But I'm afraid I've already booked your room—a reservation made well in advance, confirmed—you do understand, don't you?"

"Yes, I certainly do," she said. "Have no fear, I shall be out by check-out time."

She had half expected to find that the entire town would be closed to her, but as it turned out she found a room the second place she checked, a small, modest hotel in the downtown area. It was old-fashioned but clean and respectable looking—and not the property of the Lions family.

"I'm Mrs. Roberts, my husband and I have owned the hotel for ten years now," the woman who showed her to her room explained. "Of course, it's not as fancy as the new motels, but our guests often come back again and again, they like the homey atmosphere, they tell us."

"And I'm sure I will too," Peggy assured her.

"Oh, how long will you be staying, Miss Conners?"

Peggy hesitated. "Not too long, I hope," she said. "Let's say, a week. Is that all right?"

"No problem. Fortunately we had a cancellation on a reservation. Sometimes during the summer we're booked solid. I'll put you down for a week, then."

"Fine," Peggy said. Surely in a week's time she could accomplish what she had to accomplish.

Once settled into her new room, she strolled back to her former motel. For one thing, she wanted to leave a forwarding address. In a sense, she wanted to let Mrs. Denver know that she hadn't run away frightened; it was like throwing down the glove. Of course, she was smart enough to know that Mrs. Denver would find her anyway. It was a small town, and with the family's influence locally she would soon know Peggy was still here, and just where she was staying.

"And I do not intend to cower in my room like a frightened mouse," Peggy told herself firmly. She had another reason too for leaving her new address; Alex Lions had promised he would bring Allison to see her, and for whatever reason, she believed him. She wanted to make it as easy as possible for him to find her.

Having informed a rather nervous desk clerk where she could be found, she strolled into the coffee shop and took a seat. She had a vague hope that she might learn something more from the waitress, Sally, but she saw that as the girl approached her table, she wore a sullen expression.

"Good morning," Peggy said, smiling. The girl mumbled a greeting and slapped a menu on the table in front of her.

Peggy ordered coffee and toast, and when it was brought, she again attempted conversation. "I didn't realize when we were talking yesterday that the Lions family owns this motel," she said.

"Look," Sally said, "I don't have time to stand and chatter with customers, I'm awfully busy." With that, she hurried back in the direction of the kitchen. Peggy glanced around; at the moment she was the only customer in the place.

"Oh well," she thought with a shrug, "I might have

expected that too." She finished her coffee quickly and prepared to leave; Sally did not reappear; when a family of four came in, another girl came to serve them.

The day seemed to drag by slowly. Peggy strolled about the town for a time but, afraid that she might miss Alex and Allison, she returned to her hotel room with a paperback novel and settled in to wait. Lunchtime came and she had a sandwich and some milk sent up; then she continued to wait.

It was two in the afternoon when the knock finally came at her door. Momentarily afraid that it might be Mrs. Denver, back for yet another confrontation, she opened the door a mere crack. It was Allison. She looked angry, and petulant, the way she always looked when she had made up her mind to be as difficult as she could be about whatever it was you wanted; Peggy knew the look well. But at least it was Allison, and she was here—with Alex Lions waiting behind her.

"I'm glad you found me," she said, opening the door wide.

"They said at the motel you'd moved," Alex said. Allison said nothing, only glanced disdainfully around the plain, simply furnished room.

"Had to. I had a visit from your friend"—she glanced meaningfully at Allison—"who voiced all sorts of dire threats and insinuations and then had me tossed out, practically into the streets."

"You mean you were asked to move?" Alex looked annoyed.

"That's putting it in the politest terms," Peggy said with a wry smile.

"I'll look into it."

Allison had gone to the window to glance out. Now

100

she seated herself in the room's only chair and tossed a defiant look at Peggy. "What is this all about, anyway?" she demanded. "Alex practically dragged me in here, against my better judgment, if you want to know. This had better be good."

"It will be," Peggy promised her.

"Look," Alex said, "I promised you a chance to talk. Alone. I'll wait in the lobby."

Peggy threw him a grateful look. He nodded and went out. When the door had closed softly but firmly behind him, Peggy turned back to her sister.

"Now listen, Allison," she began.

"I am not Allison."

Peggy brought her hand down hard on the top of the dresser. She saw Allison flinch at the sound. So, she was nervous, at least; and with good reason, Peggy thought wryly.

"Stop it," she said aloud. "I don't know what sort of game you're playing, although I think I could make a pretty good guess. But I'll have no more of this pretense, not with me. Maybe you can forget all the years together, everything my family has done for you, our friendship, your place in our family—but *I* can't, and I won't. Argue with me if you must, but do not insult my intelligence any further."

"I don't know what you're talking about," Allison cried, springing up from the chair. She began to pace back and forth like a caged animal. Her hands, where they gripped her purse, were white with tension.

"Why did you come here? Why did you leave in the middle of the night, without a word? Why are you pretending to be someone else?"

"I am not pretending," Allison nearly screamed. "I

am *not* the person you're looking for. I am Melissa Gilbert. Why won't you just accept that? And leave. That's all I want of you, that's the only reason I agreed to come here today to see you, to ask you, to beg you, to leave. You don't know what you're getting into.''

''Do you?'' Peggy asked softly.

''Yes.'' But Allison's voice lacked conviction. ''Oh, don't look so, so condemning. You don't understand any of this.''

''Then make me understand. Explain it to me. I promise you I'll listen and make every attempt to understand, to see it from your point of view. Just start at the beginning, with Mrs. Denver.''

For a moment she thought Allison was going to give in and tell her. Then the girl gave her head an angry toss. ''There isn't any Mrs. Denver. Look, can't you just leave it at that, can't you just go—and leave me alone. Is that too much to ask of you?''

''Under the present circumstances, yes,'' Peggy said. Then, desperately, ''Oh, Allison, darling sister, this is not the first time you've gotten some harebrained scheme in your head and gone off half cocked to get yourself into trouble. It's exactly like that business with the doll house when you were seven, remember? Father wouldn't buy it for you, so you took it out of the store, thinking once you had it at home he would have to agree that it was yours, and it would just simply be so. Only . . .''

''This isn't like that time at all,'' Allison cried. ''That was different. I was entitled to the doll house, he'd already given you a new bicycle and . . . Oh!'' She caught herself, but too late. Peggy smiled smugly and came across the room, to grip Allison's trembling arms.

"Yes, you're right, he had given me a bicycle," Peggy said, "and in your mind that made everything different. Just as in your mind you've already found some sort of justification for what you're up to here. Now, suppose you sit down again and tell me all about it, Allison."

Chapter 13

Allison slumped into the chair, looking defeated and sullen. There was no longer any pretense, nor need of any. Between them, at least, the game was ended.

"You always think you're so damned smart," Allison said bitterly. "But just for the record, you don't know *everything*, Peggy Conners."

"I'm aware of that," Peggy said, seating herself on the bed. "But I mean to learn the rest of it. Now, just how did all this get started, anyway? Where did you meet Mrs. Denver?"

"She isn't Mrs. Denver, she's Mrs. Marvel."

"With so many names it's difficult to know which is the correct one."

"I met her at Hunter's Point, that night at dinner. She was sitting in the dining room when we came in. She told me later that she'd watched us until you left. Then she came over and asked if she could sit at our table. At first I resented the intrusion, but she began talking almost at once. It sounded so intriguing—of course, she couldn't explain everything, just enough to get me interested. And she asked me to meet her the next day, to talk more fully."

"And you got rid of me so you could meet her by the lake?"

"Yes." Allison at least had the grace to look a bit embarrassed over her subterfuge. "Oh, I hated lying to you, you know that, for heaven's sake. But she had insisted that our meeting must be utterly secret. And she'd talked about a big reward for me if things went right.

"So, I met her, and she outlined her plans. She was looking for someone to impersonate Jacob Lions long lost granddaughter. I was the right age, the right physical type, everything. And if I got away with it, there'd be a big bundle of money in it for me."

"There's one thing I don't understand," Peggy interjected. "On the terrace, how did she pick you of all the girls she might have approached?"

For the first time in their interview Allison's face brightened. "That's the really odd part of it, Peg. She said she was guided there, to that place, at that time. She said she knew that when the right girl came along, she'd be given a sign. And then she saw us come in, and order, and we had a glass of wine—Lions wine, remember? We even picked up the bottle and discussed the label. She said she knew at once that it was her sign, that it was one of us. And then, when you got up and left, leaving me alone at the table—well, you know the rest."

"No," Peggy said, "not all of it. I don't know, for instance, why you ever agreed to such a crazy scheme. Surely you must have seen that what you were agreeing to do was illegal?"

Allison shook her head disdainfully. "Illegal? What

nonsense. It's illegal when Father finds ways of taking things off his income tax that he shouldn't take. It's illegal when you drive over the speed limit, which you do all the time. And when Mother is having trouble sleeping and she borrows one of Aunt Grace's sleeping pills, that's illegal too.''

''But those are harmless things, of no real significance. Allison, don't you see, you could go to prison for what you're trying to do.''

Allison jumped up again and began pacing the floor as she had done earlier. ''No,'' she said.

''No what?''

She turned to face Peggy and now her face wore a triumphant expression. ''No, Peggy, I can't go to prison for impersonating Jacob Lions' granddaughter.''

''Don't be stupid,'' Peggy said sharply. ''You're smarter than that. Of course you can, this involves a fortune, a very large one, and fraud, and . . .''

''No,'' Allison said again, firmly. ''I can't. Because, you see, Peggy, I'm not impersonating Melissa Gilbert . . .''

''You've been living here under that name, you've gone to great lengths to convince the family members, even the sheriff . . .''

''. . . I *am* Melissa Gilbert.''

Peggy stopped short, staring. The silence grew long between them. From outside Peggy could hear the sound of midafternoon traffic. Someone was strolling past outside, whistling a tune. A fly had taken advantage of the open window and was buzzing insistently around her head.

"Allison," she said in a whisper.

"Not Allison . . . Melissa." Allison looked quite pleased with herself.

"Allison, I don't know what kind of game you're trying to play now, but I'm not buying it."

Allison crossed the room toward her; she was suddenly bursting with excitement, with enthusiasm. She had already forgotten that Peggy had tricked her confession from her, suddenly she was the old Allison, sharing some exciting piece of mischief with her sister.

"Oh, Peggy, you've got a closed mind, don't be like that. Think about it, just think about the possibility. Look, Jacob Lions lost his daughter and granddaughter in a boating accident fourteen years ago, on this same lake. The granddaughter was five. And fourteen years ago, you found me on your doorstep in Hunter's Point. Isn't that a bit much for a coincidence?"

"Hunter's Point just isn't that close to here," Peggy said, hardly able to believe what she was hearing. "A five-year-old girl—you couldn't have gotten that far without someone—the police or someone—seeing you and picking you up as a lost child."

"But you don't know how far I had to go, maybe not far at all. The boat was lost, it was never found. My mother's body was found, east of here—halfway to Hunter's Point. For all we know, I was lost—or even deliberately left—at Hunter's Point."

It was Peggy's turn to stand and pace back and forth in the narrow confines of the room. This was certainly an aspect of the situation that she had never, in her wildest imaginings, considered. Allison—Melissa?

"No, I can't believe it," she said finally, turning to face her sister. "You were five, that's old enough to remember things. And never in all these years have you had any recollection of here, of the island, of your family.''

"Amnesia," Allison said. "I couldn't remember anything, don't you see? Not this family, or any other. Something must have happened to block my memory of things."

"And now I suppose you remember it all?" Peggy said a bit drily.

Allison missed the tone. Her eyes sparkled. "Yes, truly, ever since I arrived here, things have been coming back to me, all sorts of things."

"Such as?"

"Why, even before we got to the island, I knew what it would look like, and the house too—and my grandfather, I would have recognized him anywhere, even if I'd passed him on the street."

"Perhaps because Mrs. Denver's—excuse me, Mrs. Marvel's description of him was so excellent?"

"Oh, I'll admit," Allison said, not in the least daunted by Peggy's skepticism, "at first it was just a sham, a stunt, a way to have some fun, to give the family a hard time after the rotten way everyone had treated me—and, too, a chance to make some money, so I could have a real summer vacation. But that was *before,* Peggy. Now it's not a trick or a scheme anymore. Peggy, I know, I *am* Melissa Gilbert."

"Where does Mrs. Marvel come into all this?"

"She's my grandfather's astrological advisor; he's very big on the subject. When I disappeared, you see, he spent a fortune on detectives, looking for me. As my body had never washed up, naturally . . ."

"Naturally," Peggy said.

". . . he never accepted that I was dead. And there were no heirs, you see—he'd disinherited Alex, and Jack was just a poor cousin, no one pays any real attention to him. And then Mrs. Marvel came along, Jack found her, and she's the world's greatest genius at reading the stars. And she predicted, from reading the stars, that I would reappear. And that's what kept the old man looking for me all these years."

"And when Melissa did not reappear as the stars predicted," Peggy said, "Mrs. Marvel had to manufacture a Melissa—you."

"She set out to find me by following what the stars told her to do," Allison corrected her, looking annoyed. "Oh, why won't you believe what is so obvious?"

"To you, maybe—certainly not to me. Allison, look at it this way, even if you were Melissa—and you'll never convince me of it—don't you see, you're still in a very dangerous position. From what you've told me, Mrs. Marvel is not just doing this to be kind or to help the old man. She's doing it for what she can get out of it—presumably money. Even if your identity as Melissa is established, do you think she'll allow you to inherit all the money that she has worked and schemed for? Not on your life. Once it's your money instead of old Jacob Lions', then she'll start scheming to get it from you. There's no telling what she might do."

Allison laughed softly. "There's no need. You see, we've already worked all that out. I'll get my reward—and it's very generous, too—and she'll get the rest, and we'll go our own separate ways."

"I can't believe this," Peggy said, growing angry at Allison's continued stubbornness. "You, involved in something as shoddy as this—bilking a sick old man . . .''

"I've made him happy. He hasn't got long to live anyway."

"And what if Mrs. Marvel decides that it's too long to wait?"

The quick flash of guilt on Allison's face told Peggy that Allison had faced that possibility too—and accepted it in her mind.

"There'd be no need for anything like that," she said, but she was sullen again. "I told you, he hasn't got long to live. A few weeks maybe, the doctors say."

"And you believe that once he dies Mrs. Marvel will give you your money—a sizable portion of the fortune she's schemed to get—and let you go your own way? You, the one person who knows what she's done, you, the one who could expose her as a fraud? I think not."

Allison's anger, when it came, was tinged with something else; fear, Peggy thought. Fear, because she too had considered the same question, and was far less confident of her answers than she claimed to be.

"You just won't listen," Allison cried. "I've told you the truth, the way it really is, but you've got your mind made up otherwise. Well, I don't care, there's nothing you can do about any of this, and don't try, Peggy, just don't try."

"I can go to the authorities, I can tell them everything," Peggy threatened.

Allison laughed. "What good would that do? They didn't believe you before and they won't believe you now. And you're forgetting the most important point. I *am* Melissa Gilbert. So I'm not guilty of anything. There's no crime in coming home to my grandfather."

111

"And to your inheritance?"

"Yes, that too. Why shouldn't I have it, it's mine, isn't it? You're just jealous because it isn't yours, because I've done all this on my own, without your help or the family's. Or your blessing. You've always liked to think of me as poor pathetic Allison, Allison the unknown, the unwanted, the burden. And now that I've made up my mind to be myself, you can't stand it, you want me always dependent upon you."

"Allison . . ." Peggy was shocked at this admission of how Allison had regarded their relationship all these years. She had never suspected any resentment, any unhappiness; in her mind, Allison had always been accepted and treated as a full member of the family. And yet—had they from time to time been patronizing? Had they looked upon her as a burden, as a chance to show how good, how generous they were? For a moment Peggy was forced to look into her own heart, examine her motives in an effort to weigh the possible truth of Allison's words, to discover how such bitterness had welled up in her, made her so reckless, so full of hate.

"Oh, don't look so shocked," Allison said sharply.

"I . . . I never knew."

"Of course not, because I never told you. How could I? I was dependent, at the mercy of you or your parents for everything, for a place to sleep, for the food I ate, for the clothes I wore. And there have been times—not always, not all the time—but often, I've hated you all for it."

She snatched up her purse from the bed and hurried to the door, pausing there for a final shot. "This is my big chance, my chance to be myself, to buy a life of my own, and I won't let you mess it up for me."

With that she was gone, the door slamming behind her. The sound seemed to echo in the room. Peggy felt drained. She had seen an Allison she had never known existed.

"Perhaps," she thought sadly, "because I never tried to know."

She went to the window and stared out without seeing the scene before her. Melissa; was it possible?

And now that the harsh words were over, now that she could, so to speak, take a step back and view the matter calmly, she had to admit that it was possible. Just barely, perhaps—but it was possible.

Chapter 14

Peggy was curious to know what Allison had told
Alex when she came down to the lobby. But he did not
come up or call, and although she felt disappointed she
tried to tell herself that that had not been part of the
agreement. He had promised to give her a chance to talk
to Allison and he had kept his promise.

When all was said and done, she was not sure what,
if anything, she had accomplished. She had seen Allison, and she had gotten her to admit who she was and
what she was doing. But this new scheme, or delusion,
or whatever it was, seemed to complicate things even
more.

She was at a complete loss as to what she should do
next. She knew what Allison wanted her to do, of
course; and perhaps that would be the wisest course of
action after all. Allison was not a child anymore; she
was not even a blood relation. Her only interest here
was in Allison the woman, and if Allison did not want
her interference, as she strongly did not, then maybe it
was time to leave gracefully. Certainly everyone
involved would be happier: Mrs. Marvel, Alex, Jack
Lions, the sheriff—she frowned as she thought of one

person who hadn't been consulted, the one person involved in this whole business whom she had not yet met—Jacob Lions. Would he be better off, or happier?

And yet even his welfare wasn't a valid argument against persisting in her efforts to dissuade Allison from her scheme. It was probable that old Jacob Lions was happier in his delusion than he would be if she unmasked Allison. At the moment he was knowing the pleasure of having the girl he thought to be his long-lost granddaughter returned to him. He was dying, which must make his happiness in finding her even more poignant. Would it really be a kindness on her part to take that happiness from him?

At length, confused by her ponderings, she went out to stroll about the town. She found an antique shop and picked up a charming old carved picture frame for her mother, and an old brooch for herself. In another store she bought notepaper.

And all the while the same thoughts kept churning around in her mind. In despair she went to a movie, but after sitting for two hours staring at the screen she realized she had no idea what was happening in front of her, and left. By this time it was evening, and she had a cocktail and dinner. Finally deciding to put her insistent thoughts to rest, she returned to her hotel room.

She stopped in the lobby to see if she had any messages. "No, sorry, Miss Conners, not a thing," the clerk informed her.

There was really no reason for anyone to call her, she told herself on the way up in the elevator. Alex had already heard her version of the meeting from Allison and no doubt he felt convinced that he had done his duty and been fair.

Why then should she feel this sense of disappointment? Perhaps because she had wanted something more than just fairness from him.

Although the day had been warm, there was a cool breeze blowing through her room. She went to stand at the window for a moment. As she did so, her gaze went down to the street below.

Suddenly she moved back, out of the direct line of the window. That man, standing in the doorway across the street—could it be Waldo, the chauffeur? But what would he be doing there, as if . . . as if he were spying on her?

She peered out again, more cautiously this time—but the doorway across the street was empty. The man who had been standing there, half in, half out of the shadows, had gone, whoever he had been. She looked up and down the street. Several people strolled by but there was no one she could say with certainty was the same man.

She glanced uneasily at the old fire escape that ran up the building—past her window. It would be easy for a strong, athletic man to reach the fire escape from the street—and have instant access into her room.

"Now I'm being silly," she reprimanded herself. To prove to herself that she wasn't really frightened by that prospect, she left the window open a little when she climbed into bed.

But she did not sleep easily that night. For a long while she tossed and turned and stared at the patterns of light on the ceiling. The town outside grew still as the night deepened and finally the noise of people still moving about on their business faded to the hum of an occasional automobile passing by, and once or twice the crunch of footsteps on the sidewalk below.

Yet at every strange noise she started, snapping herself back from the sleep into which she was trying to drift. Was that a sound at her door? Had those footsteps paused just below her window?

When at last she did sleep, it was to dream—not the pleasant, gentle dreams of childhood, but a shadow-haunted nightmare. She dreamed that she was running, running through a strange, eerie forest; the bushes tore at her skirt and it seemed as if the branches of the trees reached down to try to entangle her. She was in a fog, so that she could hardly see where she was going, and at first she did not know whether she was running from, or to something.

Something moved ahead of her, a shadow among the shadows, that at last took form and became a person, running ahead of her.

"Allison," she cried, recognizing the person at last, but a voice cried back to her, "I am not Allison, I am Melissa."

She looked again, and indeed it was not Allison, nor Melissa either, but Mrs. Marvel, laughing sardonically as she ran.

Peggy stopped short, but suddenly Mrs. Marvel was pursuing her, crying "I am Melissa. I am Melissa." Peggy ran, fighting her way through wisps of fog and clinging branches, and when she looked again, Waldo was there too, and Jack Lions, and Alex, and Allison, all pursuing her, each of them claiming to be Melissa.

Suddenly she tripped and fell, but she did not fall to the ground as she expected, she tumbled into an open shaft that yawned up suddenly before her. Down and down and down she fell, into a darkness that grew ever darker.

It weighed her down, seeming to crush her, and the air grew thinner and thinner, and harder to pull into her lungs. She was suffocating in the heavy, smothering darkness. She fought to breathe and could not.

And suddenly she knew, with blinding panic—it was no dream. She was awake, in her bed, and she was unable to breathe. She struggled, but something was over her, upon her, something covered her face.

A pillow! Someone was holding a pillow over her face, smothering her in her sleep. She hit out into the darkness above, striking and clawing, and struck a strong, hairy arm, a wrist. She tugged frantically at the hand holding the pillow, trying to pry it loose. Her lungs felt as if they were on fire and the darkness had begun to rock and sway with her. Searing flashes of light were exploding inside her head. But the hands holding the pillow were too powerful for her, she could not dislodge them, and she knew that she was fast losing consciousness.

She struck out with her legs, bringing a pained grunt from her assailant, but hardly loosening his hold. Her fingers clawed at the bed, the pillows, the nightstand—and caught in an electrical cord.

She yanked, hard. The lamp on the nightstand toppled, fell to the floor with a crash, taking an ashtray with it. She clutched the nightstand and pulled at it too, knocking it over with yet another crash.

The noise must have frightened her assailant. For a

119

moment he hesitated, the pressure on her face lessening. Then, even through the smothering pillow, she could hear a knocking at the door.

"Are you all right in there?" someone called out, and then, knocking louder, "Hello?"

Suddenly the pressure was gone. The pillow was still there, so it was a moment before she realized no one was holding it down anymore. She flung it away, greedily gulping air into her lungs. The room still swayed and tipped when she tried to sit up. She had a glimpse of someone disappearing out the window, but in the darkness, dazed as she was, she could say nothing more than that it was a man.

The room gradually righted itself and she became aware of the continued, increasingly insistent knocking at the door; still gasping for air she clambered from the bed and staggered across the room, flicking on the overhead light before she flung the door open.

By this time a little crowd of people had gathered, including the owner, Mrs. Roberts, and her husband. "Is anything wrong?" she asked and then, "Oh, what's happened?"

"I . . . I had an attacker," Peggy stammered, clutching her throat.

Her announcement was greeted with shock and dismay, and the people in the hall crowded into her room to observe the broken lamp and the tipped-over table, that had brought about her rescue.

"Just in the nick of time, I'd say," Mrs. Roberts said, eyeing the bed and the pillow with wide eyes.

Her husband had gone to the window to peer out,

followed by several others, as if they expected to see the attacker still waiting outside. Of course he was gone; Peggy knew that. But would he be back?

"Did you get a look at him?" Mr. Roberts asked, coming back into the room.

She shook her head. "No, it was dark and I was too stunned." She did not voice her suspicions as to who it might have been; they were only suspicions after all; and just now she didn't want to cause any more trouble in that quarter.

"I'll call the police," Mrs. Roberts said, moving purposefully toward the hall.

"No, that isn't necessary," Peggy said quickly. The hotel owner looked surprised, but Peggy was firm. "There's no point in it really, he's gone, and he surely won't come back. And I couldn't identify him anyway, so nothing would come of it."

"Well . . ." Mrs. Roberts, trying not to look relieved, glanced indecisively toward her husband. Of course they would be glad to avoid any further disturbance; to call in the police in the middle of the night because a guest had been attacked would not do their reputation any good.

"Nothing like this has ever happened here before," he said, waiting for some further indication as to what he should do.

"And probably never will again," Peggy said. "Look, I'm all right, really. If you would just make sure the window is locked—just to be safe."

He hurried to lock the window while Mrs. Roberts shooed everyone else out of the room.

"You're sure you're all right, now," he said, pausing on his way out. "I can call a doctor for you if you like."

"No, I feel fine now," she said. It was true; although she was still a little weak, she was otherwise fine.

At last they were gone and she could sink wearily into the room's only chair, and try to think calmly about what had happened.

"Someone tried to kill me," she thought—or had they? Had they only tried to frighten her away, as Mrs. Marvel had attempted to do before with her threats?

She closed her eyes and at once remembered that awful, numbing pressure, that moment in which she had felt herself sinking. If she hadn't toppled the lamp and the nightstand over, would he have stopped, content to scare her? Or would it have gone on and on, until . . . She shuddered at the thought.

Chapter 15

She was grateful to see the sun pouring through the window and to realize that she had slept the rest of the night without any further incident. For a moment she even ignored the ringing of the telephone; at length it penetrated her awareness and she reached sleepily for the receiver. The sleepiness fled, however, when she recognized Alex Lions' voice; strange, she had spoken so little with him and yet the timbre of his voice was as immediately familiar as if she had known him for years.

"I wanted a chance to talk to you again," he was saying. "Are you free this evening?"

"Yes, of course."

"Good. Maybe we could have dinner then?" He said this impersonally, as if arranging a business meeting, nothing more. Still, she could not help a little flutter of excitement.

"That would be fine," she answered him. "Around seven. Great. See you then."

Shortly before seven she came down to the lobby to meet him. She had dressed with care, picking a robin'segg blue dress that was full and flowing and utterly feminine; she hoped that, at least, would offset the impression she must have made when they'd met on the estate and she'd looked like a drowned rat. She wore no jewelry but the old brooch she had picked up the day before; the stones, sapphire colored, picked up the shade of her eyes quite flatteringly, she thought.

She had hardly stepped into the lobby when she saw him come in from the street. He glanced quickly around, his eyes lighting on her; for a moment she thought he looked both surprised and pleased by what he saw, but his face quickly went blank and when he came over to greet her his manner was briskly impersonal.

His car, parked at the curb in front, was a small, modest sedan—a far cry from the family Rolls-Royce. There was, in fact, very little about Alex Lions to indicate that his was a very wealthy background. He had impeccable manners when he chose to display them, and the sort of inbred confidence that can come from being raised in wealth. But there was nothing showy about him; even his clothes, though good and neat, were no more expensive than those the average young man would be likely to wear, and when he took a cigarette from his pocket, asking her first if she minded, she saw that it came from a crumpled pack and not an expensive case.

"There's a little place outside of town," he said, driving with deceptive ease through the heavy traffic. "The food's good and we'll be able to talk freely."

The restaurant was unpretentious but comfortable. Alex had apparently been there often enough to be known and they were led to a booth in a back corner, very much off to themselves.

He ordered cocktails for them—a dry martini for himself, a vermouth cassis for her—and for dinner the prime rib, rare.

"The house specialty," he assured her. "Don't worry, you'll like it."

"I'm sure I shall."

When their drinks had been served and the waitress had retreated, he made his first reference to her meeting the day before with Allison.

"I trust everything was resolved to your satisfaction," he said.

"I wish it were," Peggy replied, "but we seem to be at an impasse."

"In other words, you still insist she *is* Allison," he said.

"Oh, she admitted *that* to me." His eyebrows went up; Allison, apparently, had not given him a full report of the conversation. "The problem is, she still insists that she's Melissa as well."

She told him briefly of their interview, how she had tricked Allison into admitting her identity, and of Allison's insistence that she was really the heiress who had disappeared so many years before.

"The worst of it is," she said, "that as much as I argue with her I can't help but admit the possibility that she could be right. It's far-fetched, but it is nonetheless possible."

"She certainly had me convinced she was the real thing," Alex said thoughtfully, sipping his drink. "There are so many things she knows, things no one but Melissa should have known."

"The thing I don't know," Peggy said, "is, exactly what does she stand to gain? Oh, I know, she inherits some money—but just how much money?"

"All of it. The entire Lions fortune. As soon as Father was convinced who she was, she was in line for everything."

Peggy was surprised and showed it; she had never dreamed how amibitious their scheme was. She said, "Then you of all people should be interested in discrediting her, I should think. Doesn't that mean she's going to get your portion too?"

"I have no portion, not in the Lions estate," he said drily. "I was disinherited years ago."

"Oh. I see." She was embarrassed at having drawn such personal information from him but he shrugged it off as if it were of no consequence.

"No need to be embarrassed about it, I'm not," he said easily. "I was engaged to a girl my father didn't consider suitable. He told me if I persisted in the engagement he would disinherit me, and when I persisted, he did as he threatened."

"And the girl?"

He smiled a bit ruefully. "When she found out I was no longer heir to the Lions fortune, she disinherited me too."

"I'm sorry."

"Don't be." He sounded quite unconcerned. "It was years ago and I was young and foolish. But I had too much pride to accept my father's sympathy when it happened. I told him I had no desire for him to change his will again. All I asked was to be given the French vineyards to manage—they were new for us then—and to be treated like any other employee, allowed to make

126

my own way. He agreed and I went abroad. I've lived there most of the time since, except for a few visits home.''

''I see,'' Peggy said. This explained a great deal, such as why he looked like a workman and not a wealthy scion; and why he lived in such a practical fashion, without the expensive clothes and fabulous cars that she had expected of him.

''Was this before Melissa's disappearance?'' she asked.

''Yes. I came home then, of course, for a time, but there simply wasn't much I could do, and the French vineyards needed me badly just then, so I went back.''

''What exactly happened, anyway? I know there was an accident, a boating accident.''

He shrugged and said, ''That's about as much as I can tell you. When I went to France my sister, Claire, was widowed and living with her daughter, Melissa, at the house. Claire was very independent, headstrong, but she was devoted to my father, and she helped a great deal with the business. Apparently, though, they had a quarrel, and Claire decided she was going to go out in the boat to cool off. There was a storm coming up but that didn't dissuade Claire, nor even prevent her from taking little Melissa along. They went out—and never came back. They found the boat eventually, and after a time, Claire's body. That was when I came back. But they never found Melissa's body. I always believed she drowned too; it seemed so unlikely that she could have made it to shore when Claire hadn't.''

''But your father always believed that she was alive.''

"Yes." He frowned thoughtfully. "But that was Mrs. Marvel's doing."

They were interrupted by the arrival of the waitress with their dinner and for a few minutes their attention was diverted from the subject of Melissa. The food was as good as Alex had promised and Peggy was surprised to find that she was quite hungry.

"Mrs. Marvel arrived after Melissa's disappearance, is that right?" she asked finally when the edge was gone from her appetite.

"Yes. I wasn't here then either. I don't even know exactly when she did come, I just remember a reference to her on one of my father's letters. His new advisor, he called her. It was a long while before I knew that she was his personal astrologer."

"Were you shocked?"

"Not particularly. Father had always been keen on things of that sort. I'll admit I was a little surprised to find he'd hired his own personal stargazer, that seemed a little far out, but at the time I didn't think it could do much harm."

"But it did, you mean?"

"Unfortunately, yes."

"You mean about Melissa, making him believe Melissa might be alive?"

"That was part of it. And it was stated not as a possibility, but as a fact. Apparently that was her introductory card, she came to him with the news that she had learned from the stars that Melissa was alive and would come back to him."

"But the stars didn't say exactly when."

He nodded and said, "That's right. But he was so pleased by her news that he accepted it, and everything else she said. She started advising him in other things, every detail of his personal life—and business matters as well.''

''And that's the other unfortunate part, I suppose,'' Peggy prompted him.

''Yes. I had no idea things were going downhill the way they were. I suppose Father's judgment started going bad as his health deteriorated. Anyway, I gradually began picking up on some of the errors, even from where I was. And since I've been back, I've been discovering how bad—and how widespread—they really are. I'd have come back sooner, only I didn't know he was as sick as he was. He never mentioned it, and no one else troubled to tell me. All the people who were here when I was around, who might have gotten in touch with me, were gone. Everyone on the island now has been hired since Mrs. Marvel came—presumably on her advice.''

''I see—this beef is delicious, by the way.''

''I'm glad you're enjoying it. Coffee?''

He ordered coffee for each of them and sat back in the booth, more relaxed than she had yet seen him. Peggy finished the last morsel of baked potato and smiled her approval at him.

When the coffee was brought and their plates cleared, she went back to the subject at hand. ''What about Jack? Where does he fit into the scheme of things?''

Alex seemed to regard Jack as of little consequence. ''Oh, Jack's always been the family black sheep. He's only vaguely connected with the family, anyway—a stepsister of father's, her illegitimate child—that sort of thing. Anyway, he came around years ago, and Father

129

took him in. But Jack's always been a bit of a recluse, he has his own apartment in the house, keeps to himself. I don't suppose I've talked to him, really talked to him, more than a half dozen times in the years I've known him. For the rest it's been hello and good-bye in passing."

"Might he be involved in Mrs. Marvel's scheme?"

"He could be, I don't suppose he stands to get much any other way. But it seems unlikely. He's such a namby-pamby."

She thought of Jack Lions as she had met him. He had not seemed such a namby-pamby then, to her. But then Alex had not been around at the time. She could well understand that around his cousin, who was dynamic, confident, forceful, Jack Lions might fade a bit, might step back into the shadows and out of the spotlight. But away from Alex, free to exercise his own sort of control—no, she did not think Jack Lions was necessarily so insignificant.

"There's just one other thing I wonder about," she said after a pause. "If you were disinherited, what would have happened to all the Lions' money had Melissa not shown up?"

"I wasn't sure of that myself until I finally got it out of Father. It seems that, despite all Mrs. Marvel's advice to the contrary, he had finally given up hope of finding Melissa. He had decided to make a new will, leaving a modest settlement for me, for Jack, and for Mrs. Marvel—and by far the largest sum to a research foundation that he's been connected with."

"And that was the catalyst needed to set Mrs. Marvel off," Peggy mused aloud. "If she allowed him to go through with that, she'd get a few crumbs, but if she provided Melissa—particularly a Melissa under her control—she stood to gain a fortune."

"Interesting situation, isn't it?" He signaled the waitress to bring them a check. "It's getting late. We'd better get going. We have important things to do.

"We? Important things?" she asked, surprised.

"Well I'll tell you the truth," he said, counting out money, "at this point in time I'm completely confused as to what the real situation is. I figure the only way I can learn whether Melissa is Melissa or Allison is Allison is to bring all the ingredients together, bring the pot to a boil, and give it a good stir."

"Which means what, exactly?"

He came around to help her out of the booth, and she found herself being hurried along by his hand at her elbow.

"It means I know only one way of getting everyone involved together. You and I are going to Lions Island. After stopping at your hotel, of course."

"But why my hotel?"

He stopped just outside the door. "So you can pack, of course. If you're coming out to stay on the island, you won't need a hotel room too."

Chapter 16

It was the first time she had ever actually come up to the house, whose rooftop she had seen several times from the distance. How different it was this time to tie up at the landing with Alex, and not have to be afraid of encountering him—or anyone else.

Yet how sorry she was to see that boat ride end. When he had decided she should move to the island she had been too surprised to give much thought to the fact that she would be with him. There was the quick trip back to town, the hurried packing while he waited in the lobby. She had to turn her head away so the desk clerk would not see her giggling at his shocked expression.

And then, they were in the boat, alone in the darkness, cutting through the water toward Lions Island—and suddenly she had become again aware of him, close to her, drawing her into the circle of his magnetic attraction. She had shivered and he, seeing it, had thought that she was cold from the night air.

"Come here," he said.

She went to sit by him and to her surprise his arm had come around her. For a moment she had sat stiffly, frightened by the intensity of her reaction; then she had melted against him, and suddenly he was kissing her, and her heart was pounding in her breast.

It had seemed to last forever, that kiss, as they floated through darkness, through the night, something singing within her, some sense of joy that she had never before discovered within herself. Was it cold? Had it started to rain? Was there a world out there, beyond the confines of this space they shared? She neither knew nor cared.

But at last the world intruded. A wave made the boat tilt dizzily and his attention was brought back to it. It had begun to rain while he piloted the little boat safely in to the landing. He continued to hold her, but made no attempt to kiss her again, or verbally acknowledge the feelings that had sparked between them.

"Usually there's a cart here to drive up to the house," he said apologetically, looking into the boathouse. "But it looks like we'll have to hoof it tonight or wait down here till it stops raining."

She had no objection to spending the time in the boathouse with him, but she sensed that he was impatient now to get to the house, to carry through this scheme of his to its conclusion. Now that she was actually here, and partly free of the spell that his kiss had cast over her, she had begun to feel a bit nervous. She had seen the glint of excitement in his eyes and she had an uneasy suspicion that his passion in the boat had been partly an expression of his sense of excitement at the showdown to come.

"I don't mind the walk," she said. "And it's barely sprinkling now."

It was only a five-minute walk up to the main house. For the first time Peggy was able to pass safely through the Lions' gate. As she did so, she glanced up involuntarily at the stone beasts. They seemed to scowl down fiercely upon her, no more welcoming, nor less threatening, than they had been before.

"*Beware, we stand at the gates of hell,*" the inscription warned her. She shuddered.

"Cold again?" Alex asked, his arm again encircling her shoulders. But this time the warmth of his embrace couldn't dispel the chill within.

The drive curved about a stand of trees; before them, suddenly, was the house, a massive Victorian mansion with fanciful turrets and gables, fairly drooping under the weight of ornate gingerbread carving. A columned porch ran across the front and on either side was white latticework, open in a giant circle in the center. They entered the porch through the circular opening.

A thick, awkward woman in a maid's uniform came along the hall toward them as they entered the house. She stopped, surprised, when she saw Peggy with Alex.

"Good evening, Mrs. Brunner," Alex greeted her. "This is Miss Conners. She's come to spend a few days with us. Would you prepare a room for her?"

After a lengthy pause, during which Peggy half expected the servant to refuse his request, she said, "It's short notice."

"Anything will do," Peggy said quickly. "I don't want to cause a lot of trouble."

The resentful eyes watching her seemed to say, "Then you shouldn't have come at all." But the maid only nodded and went the other way, toward the stairs that led upward at the end of the hall.

"Waldo's wife," Alex said in a whisper, and she nodded; that explained everything, she thought. She could hardly imagine most people being comfortable in a house with servants like those two. But then, Mrs. Marvel was not like other people, and Allison—well, Allison had her reasons for being contented.

"If there's anyone about, they'll be in here," Alex said, leading her to an archway that opened onto a vast parlor filled with heavy, dark furniture. At one end of the room a fire flickering in a huge fireplace tried feebly to dispel the room's gloom. There was no one here either.

"I think we could use a drink after that rain," he said. "Brandy?"

"Sounds good." She gazed about the room. It was not a comfortable room, nor a comforting one. She supposed it had remained unchanged in appearance since the house had first been built; she could well understand that Alex would be more comfortable living elsewhere.

"Don't worry," he said, bringing her a glass filled with amber liquid, "it isn't *all* this bad."

"It is pretty grim, isn't it?" she said, smiling.

They both froze as they heard the sound of footsteps in the hall, not Mrs. Brunner's heavy tread, but a lighter, more youthful step.

"Alex, Mrs. Brunner said . . ." Allison came into the room and stopped, staring at them. She was wearing a white silk blouse and jodhpurs and she looked very much the young aristocrat, the landed gentry. How quickly she changed, Peggy thought fleetingly, how easily she absorbed all this—as if she were born to it.

"Hello, Allison," she said tensely, trying to sound friendly.

"I thought we had all that out yesterday," Allison said coolly.

"Apparently not to everyone's satisfaction," Alex informed her.

Allison turned on him as if Peggy were not even in the room. "Why did you bring her here?" she demanded angrily.

"Because I want to find out the truth, and it seemed like the best way to do that was to get everyone together in one time and place."

Allison's gaze went from one to the other of them. Then she said "We'll see what Mrs. Marvel has to say about that," and turned to leave.

"There's one thing you'd better get used to," Alex said in a voice that was all the more menacing for being so soft and low, "Mrs. Marvel is no boss of mine. As far as I'm concerned, she is only an employee of my father's, and not a very satisfactory one at that."

Allison turned back at the archway to glower at him. "More than an employee," she said. "A friend of mine as well. And there's one thing you'd better get used to, Alex Lions, you count for nothing here. So long as my grandfather remains alive, you are his son and an employee; but when he goes, you will be nothing more than an employee, and not a very satisfactory one either."

With that she went out of the room; they heard her heels clicking once more along the hallway.

Peggy cast an apprehensive glance at Alex. She could see that he was infuriated by Allison's cruel reminder of his own tenuous position in the house. She knew that beneath his usual composure he was a man of violent feelings. What would it be like if those passions were released, especially if they were directed toward herself? He would be devouring in love—and terrifying in hate.

"Welcome to Lions' house," he said drily, tilting his glass. She sipped more thoughtfully and made no answer; none seemed to be called for. The chill of the room had increased despite the fire in the fireplace.

Mrs. Brunner returned shortly. Peggy was glad to see her; since Allison's brief and spiteful appearance, all the charm had fled from the evening. Alex had grown withdrawn and morose, and she could not guess what bitter thoughts occupied his mind as he stared into the fire, seemingly unaware of her presence.

"I have a room ready," Mrs. Brunner announced. "It is short notice, so you'll have to make allowances."

"I'm sure it will be fine," Peggy said. She had only the one bag—the rest of her things were still at the cottage at Hunter's Point—and Mrs. Brunner seized that up as if afraid Peggy might have some other plans for it. Alex responded curtly to Peggy's "good night," and with an increasing sense of apprehension, Peggy followed the housekeeper from the room and up the shadowy stairs at the end of the hall.

The house had electricity, but it had apparently been installed many years before, and sparingly. Only one dim light showed their way up the stairs, and the hall, and Mrs. Brunner led her directly to it.

It was a small room but not much more cozy than the parlor below. The ceiling was high, lost in shadows somewhere above. The bed was a massive fourposter, hung with heavy velvet draperies, and the other furniture—bureaus, chests, an armoire—were equally dark and heavy. As below, a fire had been quickly started in the fireplace and now it bravely tried to hold back the encroaching shadows.

"Shall I unpack for you?" Mrs. Brunner asked coldly.

"That won't be necessary," Peggy said. "And thank you for your trouble. I know I was unexpected."

"We do not often have guests," Mrs. Brunner said. "Good night, miss."

The door closed solidly after her. Peggy sighed and glanced around once more. She shuddered to think what nightmares a room like this might inspire.

A check revealed that the windows, two in one wall, overlooked the lawn and the distant vineyards. She was glad to see that they opened onto a plain, sheer wall; no one could gain entry to her room from a balcony. She was glad too for the lock on the door. But when she explored the connecting bathroom—an amusingly old-fashioned one—she found that it connected on the other side to a seemingly empty bedroom whose furniture was still covered in dust sheets. The white forms looked like so many waiting ghosts; the image brought back in force all her uneasiness.

It had seemed so much simpler when Alex had suggested it. But now, alone in this dreadful room, all of her doubts and fears returned to assail her. She found herself remembering that the night before someone had broken into her hotel room and tried to smother her with a pillow, either to kill her, or to frighten her. And chances were that that same someone had come from this island, from this house. She had no illusions that

Mrs. Marvel would take readily to her presence in the house. Allison certainly had not, and Jack Lions, if he had any opinion at all, would undoubtedly side with Mrs. Marvel, since his fortunes seemed to be tied to hers. And the servants, as Alex had said, had all been employed by Mrs. Marvel, and were likely to reflect her opinion.

That left only Alex, and for all his moments of tender passion he seemed to her as yet a very tentative ally; he had not yet indicated that he fully accepted her story regarding Allison, but was giving her a chance to prove it. If she could do so to his satisfaction she felt he would be strong, even tireless in unraveling the threads of mystery that surrounded Allison's presence here. But if she failed . . . what then?

Of one thing she was certain, everyone else in this house would be determined to see that she failed; everyone with one possible exception, the one man whose presence dominated the house, the island, and yet whom she had not yet met, who remained perhaps the greatest enigma of all—old Jacob Lions.

How would he react to her being here? Melissa had been a favorite of his, and for years the hope that he would find her again had been the main influence of his life. Even if her ''return'' proved to be nothing more than a fraud, how would he react to such a harsh truth, old and sick as he was? Would he prefer to cling to his illusion?

She undressed slowly for bed, wondering if she had done the right thing, to thrust herself into the jaws of the dilemma in this fashion. Jaws that at any moment might close fatally upon her.

Chapter 17

Surprisingly, her first night in that gloomy old house Peggy slept beautifully. The combination of the cool, fresh air, the distant sound of the water on the rocks, and the memory of Alex's kiss, overcame the fear inspired by the events of the previous night and by the gloomy old house.

She woke late to the golden splash of sunshine spilling through her window, making the room seem less forbidding than it had the night before. Now it was just a funny old room, not entirely lacking in a kind of nostalgic charm.

By the time she had cleaned up and dressed and come downstairs, Alex was gone—probably out working in that disordered office, Peggy thought. Mrs. Brunner, whom she met on the stairs, informed her that there was coffee in the dining room, and offered to prepare her breakfast.

"Just some toast will be fine," Peggy said. "Is Alli—Melissa around?"

"Miss Melissa generally sleeps late in the mornings," Mrs. Brunner informed her.

Just like the old Allison, Peggy thought, but did not

give voice to this. She did not ask for Mrs. Marvel either; one hoped she liked to sleep late too.

To her surprise it was Jack who waited in the dining room, giving the impression he had been hanging about until she got up. He wore the seemingly omnipresent sunglasses and he looked paler than before, as if he had been ill—or very worried.

He greeted her in a friendly enough fashion even managing a somewhat wry grin. "You seem fresh this morning," he said, holding her chair for her. "I surmise no one came into your room with an axe."

She wondered if that remark were an oblique reference to the pillow incident in her hotel room; did he know about that? Was he trying to test her, even to warn her subtly that there might be worse in store for her here?

"I slept like a log, thank you," was all she said.

"The air here is very good," he said, pouring her coffee for her without asking. "That's why I stay, although, at that, there has been a deterioration in the air even here over the last few years. These days there's hardly any place one can go and feel safe."

"And you do feel safe here?" she asked.

He smiled at that and said, "Well, yes, from the standpoint of the air I breathe at least. But as for whether it's safe for everyone, that's another matter."

"Meaning, it might not be safe for me," she said.

"Sugar?" he asked, handing the bowl across to her. "Of course, your situation here is a great deal different from mine. I live a quiet life, a withdrawn life, I keep very much to myself and rarely mix in anyone else's business."

"And yet you've come to have breakfast with me."

He shrugged; "I am like an insect, small, insignificant, fragile even—but still I am drawn to the flower's beauty. When I heard that our table was to be graced by your presence, I could not bear to stay away."

She laughed despite herself. The compliment was so old-fashioned, so extravagant, that it was hard to take it seriously; and yet, there was a glow on his face, a lingering of his hand on her arm when he touched her, that made her suspect his interest in her might be of a physical nature.

"I can only say that if I've succeeded in prying you from a hermit's life, then I feel that I've done some good by coming," she returned good-naturedly.

"Others may be sorry to see me among them." He said this in such a self-deprecating way that she could not be sure if he was serious or not. "I hardly fancy that Miss Melissa enjoys my company."

A sudden recollection flashed through her, of seeing Jack and Melissa together in the Rolls-Royce. She very nearly challenged his remark, then caught herself. Just now he seemed in a friendly, even a talkative mood, and it would be best, she thought, to take advantage of it if she could.

"And what about you?" she asked, taking a sip of coffee.

He grew suddenly wary. "What do you mean?"

She smiled to try to put him at his ease again. "What do you think of Melissa?"

"Oh, you mean, do I believe she is Melissa?" He seemed to relax again. "Why, there's no doubt of it, I knew her the moment she stepped into the room. Don't forget, I knew her as a child."

"Yes, but that was years ago," Peggy said, leaning across the table. "A girl changes a great deal between five and nineteen. How can you be so sure?"

He seemed abnormally annoyed at her persistence; perhaps this intense nervousness was what had made such a recluse of him.

"Good heavens, because I am sure," he said petulantly, sounding almost womanish. "There are things you just know. I was extremely fond of my cousin and her little girl. When Claire . . . when she was lost like that, well, I can't tell you what it did to me, I was shattered for weeks, I could hardly eat. I wonder that I even survived it myself. And like her grandfather, I never stopped believing that little Melissa would come back to us, it was the dream that kept us both alive. I would have known at once if this girl were an impostor; no one could have deceived the kind of love that I kept in my heart for that little girl."

Peggy was quite unmoved by this protestation. She was more inclined to think that Jack Lions would be incapable of really loving anyone but himself. She had known men like him before, completely wrapped up in themselves. Oh, they were capable of physical love— she had no doubt that he did find her attractive and, if encouraged, would act accordingly. But his heart was his own alone.

"Of course, if it were to your advantage," she needled him, curious to see what response it would provoke, "it might be easier to be mistaken."

To her surprise, he laughed. "You are very stubborn, as well as very desirable," he said, pushing back his chair and standing. "But there is one thing you overlook, or perhaps you don't know. There is no advantage to me one way or the other. Whatever happens, my uncle has assured me that a small trust fund has been set aside for me, a modest allowance. Whether Melissa was ever found or not had no effect on those arrangements, and her return now cannot alter them either.''

"But if you cooperated with Mrs. Marvel—if she had promised you something more . . .''

To her surprise the smile left his face and his look turned dark and angry. "Mrs. Marvel,'' he said, almost spitting the name at her. "I'll tell you this and you can believe it or not, as you wish. I hate Mrs. Marvel. I utterly despise her. She's ruined my life, she . . .''

"How has she ruined your life?'' a man's voice asked.

It was Alex, who had just come in from the hall. Jack flashed him an angry look. Then, without another word, he rushed past Alex and out of the room. Staring after him, Peggy was still startled by the intensity of feeling he had expressed. One thing was obvious to her, he had been telling the truth at the end; he hated Mrs. Marvel, hated her passionately. But could he, if he hated her like that, be in a partnership with her?

"I . . . I do seem to have set him off,'' Peggy said to Alex, smiling a bit nervously.

"It's easy to do, I'm afraid,'' he said. He came in and helped himself to some coffee. Mrs. Brunner entered from the kitchen with toast and fresh rolls, then disappeared again wordlessly.

"But why does he hate Mrs. Marvel so? They've lived in this same house apparently for years, you would think if she was that difficult, he'd have gone long ago.''

"Except he has nowhere else to go, and he's too spineless to just go out and fend for himself. But as to hating her, that seems to be mutual. They avoid each other like the plague. He never comes down to a meal with the family unless he hears ahead of time that she's not going to be there. But they both refuse absolutely to discuss the matter."

"How strange," Peggy said, biting absentmindedly into one of the rolls.

"Now," he said, looking and sounding like the Alex of the restaurant and the boat last night, "I came in specifically to find you. I thought maybe for a while at least you'd like to put aside all this commotion and disagreement and have a look around our little world."

"It sounds lovely," she said enthusiastically, her spirits lifting again. "For once I can see it without skulking around in the dark."

"I think you'll find it a great deal more interesting this way," he said.

They went out through the rear of the house. In daylight she could see that in addition to the house proper there were three large buildings.

"That farthest one is where we press the grapes," Alex explained. "The smaller one is our bottling area, and also where we work on blends, and this last building is office and storage for the bottled wines. Those that have to age or ferment in the bottles wait here as well."

"Do all of your grapes come from this area?" From here she could look up a hillside planted in vines.

"Good heavens no. We have about three hundred acres along the lake shore, in three locations, and about a hundred acres on one of the islands."

"I didn't know there was a wine industry in southern Ohio as well."

"That's really where it started," he said, opening a gate that led into the vineyards. "For years American settlers tried to grow European wine-grapes. The market for wine was here. As far back as 1694 the state of South Carolina offered a reward to the man who could produce a good native wine, but the local vines, resistant to disease and already growing here, were overlooked in favor of European cuttings that inevitably succumbed to disease or the unfriendly climate.

"It wasn't until 1802 that a man named Major John Adlum discovered the Catawba grape growing wild in his garden and decided to try making some wine from it. Eventually he sent samples to Thomas Jefferson, who thought highly of it. But more important, he sent some to a man named Nicholas Longworth in Cincinnati. Longworth became the grandfather of winemaking in Ohio. He planted his first vineyard in 1823 and in 1842, independently of French producers, he discovered champagne—actually he called it Sparkling Catawba. It was a great success. Longfellow wrote a poem to it and at one time there were complaints of French champagnes being relabeled and fraudulently passed off as authentic Sparkling Catawba."

They were among the vines now. It was still early in the season, and the grapes were no more than tiny clusters of green. Here and there silent men passed along the rows, weeding, examining the plants, she supposed, for disease, or to check their growth "What happened to that early success?" she asked.

"Disease—mostly rot, wiped out the crops. Land values rose and killed other vineyards. The wine industry virtually disappeared in the southern part of the state, but fortunately by then it had been started here—my family was one of the first to plant vineyards here. The lake climate proved to be more favorable, the warm waters provided a longer growing season for one thing. For years there was a flourishing industry here. The Victory Hotel at Put-in-Bay was the world's largest at that time, and had the first swimming area where men and women swam together—very daring at that time. But prohibition nearly killed the wine industry. Only a few survived. Fortunately, we were among them.''

He paused among the vines. ''These are Catawba grapes,'' he said. ''They could be called Ohio's own wine grape. Over there, past that marker, are Concords and a few Niagaras and Ives—all native American grapes, and becoming increasingly rare.''

''Are all American wines now made from the local grapes?'' Peggy asked.

Alex shook his head and sighed. ''No, it's pretty confusing as a matter of fact. California wines are produced from European cuttings; they took to that soil and climate, as they didn't here. And eventually French hybrids were produced that adapted to this climate too, so that many Ohio and New York wineries now grow them instead of local grapes. And to further complicate matters, France suffered an outbreak of mildew in the 1860s, and imported native American cuttings, which were resistant to disease. They were grafted onto the French vines. So there's a little American blood in the European wines you drink.''

''Are things still bleak for the local wineries?''

''They're looking better—new acreage being planted, new wineries opening, especially the little, family-operated ones. The Ohio wine industry is at a crossroads right now; and so is the Lions winery. I've had a great many fights with my father, trying to make him move more with the times.''

They had come to the building where the grapes were pressed. He led her inside, showing her the presses, including some antique ones.

"Lions is an old-fashioned house, noted for the high quality of its product. Everything here is done by hand. Whereas the larger winemakers ferment champagne in tanks, ours is still fermented in the bottle. Everything here is done by hand, the picking, the pressing—that maintains our reputation, but keeps prices up.''

"And you want to modernize?''

They went on through to the next building, where the bottling was done.

"To some extent, yes. I'd like to maintain a prestige line, hand produced, and at the same time convert to modern techniques for the bulk of our wines, to produce a more competitive wine. Just as I finally persuaded my father that we could produce both wines made from the local grapes and new ones from the French hybrids—it took me five years to talk him into that—or this, this is one of my brain children.''

He lifted a bottle from a shelf and handed it to her. "Our pure, natural line,'' he explained. "It contains no additives, no preservatives, and is fermented using only the yeasts which occur naturally on the fruit— risky, because of the greater chance of bad batches. But it's gone over well, with the same customers who look for organically grown foods.''

He handed her a bottle of champagne. "Our finest product,'' he said. "Handmade, almost a lost art. By the time that bottle gets on this shelf, it's been handled over two hundred times. Eventually, no one will be able to afford to produce wine that way—we lose money on every bottle we sell.''

''But why, at the high prices one pays in stores?''

''Taxes, for one thing. A gallon of table wine carries seventeen cents in federal tax and twenty-four cents in State tax; but champagne is taxed on the federal level at $3.40 a gallon, and another $1.25 in state taxes.''

''Pricing it out of reach of the average consumer,'' Peggy added.

''Exactly. Old-fashioned wines like this are only a labor of love. I'd like Lions to keep them, in modest quantities. But to survive, we'll have to go twentieth century. Lions, and the Ohio wine industry, will eventually either find their place in the mainstream of American wines, or fall by the wayside.''

''What will happen to the Lions winery when your father passes on?''

He smiled and said, ''That, to be sure, will be a disappointment to Melissa. The winery can't be sold, and I can't be fired. When Father dies, I'm in sole control; the business, and the money, will belong to her, but I'll run the operation.''

Apparently Allison was unaware of this, judging from her remarks the night before; and Peggy did not think she would be particularly pleased when she learned of it.

They spent a bit more time touring the facilities, and Peggy was persuaded to sample one or two of the family wines.

''Most of the wineries around here conduct tours; we never have,'' Alex explained. ''Father always felt that

150

that sort of thing got in the way of winemaking, at least for a small operation like ours, and in that I agree with him. Making great wine is a work of art; a man can't do that and act as tour guide too.''

It was nearly lunch time when they came back into the house. For the morning at least Peggy had all but forgotten the troubles that had brought her here. But as they stepped into the gloomy main hall of the house, she was reminded of them again. Mrs. Brunner, hearing their voices, came into the hall to greet them.

''Your father is awake,'' she said to Alex, ignoring Peggy. ''He's been asking about you.''

''I'll go to see him,'' Alex said.

''No,'' Mrs. Brunner said, stopping him. ''Not you. He wants to see her.'' She jerked her head in Peggy's direction.

Chapter 18

She found that she was trembling by the time she had reached the door to the old man's room. Alex, who had come to show her the way, put a hand comfortingly on her shoulder.

"I'll come in with you," he said.

"No," she said, screwing up her courage, "That won't be necessary. After all, I don't want him to think I'm a coward."

He gave her an encouraging smile. "His bark is far worse than his bite, if that's any consolation."

"Thanks," she said, and tapped lightly at the door. A gruff voice barked, "Come in," and she stepped into a cool, dark bedroom. She had a final glimpse of Alex's concerned face before she softly closed the door.

Jacob Lions was seated near the window, but the curtains were closed and the embracing wings of the thronelike chair shielded him from what little light there was, so that Peggy had to walk to stand directly in front of him before she could really see what he looked like.

The lordly face that stared at her from the shadows increased the feeling of standing before a throne. He had the keen, penetrating eyes of a hawk; the nose dominated a hard, ruggedly chiseled face that illness had not robbed of its strength; even in youth this could not have been a handsome face, but certainly a compelling, intimidating one.

He wore a monklike robe that left only his face and his hands, one resting on each arm of the chair, in view. She saw that his hands, too, though veined and gnarled, had been powerful hands, the hands of a workman and not an effete aristocrat. Like Alex's hands, she could not help thinking, and this thought drew her to the old man even though his aloof, commanding attitude held her at a distance.

For a full minute he did not speak, but only continued to stare at her in a penetrating manner. At length, determined that she would not be intimidated by him, she spoke first.

"Mrs. Brunner said you wanted to see me."

He nodded, but continued his silence for another few moments. Finally he spoke, and his voice was the quavering ghost of the resonant instrument it must once have been.

"They tell me you claim to be Melissa's sister," he said, fixing her with his wizened eyes. "But you don't look like her at all."

"Neither do you look like her," she could not help replying. "In my case, it's simple to explain. Allison— the girl you call Melissa—is not my real sister, she's adopted. We . . . we found her when she was a little girl."

"You found her when I lost her," he said. He waited, expecting her to challenge that statement, but it was ground that she had already been over with Allison, to no avail. She didn't believe that was what had happened, but she could not prove it.

At length he asked, "Why have you come here?"

"I came to find my sister, who disappeared mysteriously," Peggy said. "And I have stayed because I am afraid she is in trouble."

The old man seemed agitated by that answer. He moved as if he would rise from the chair, but his strength permitted him to do no more than brace his hands against the chair's arms.

"She's is my granddaughter. She will inherit my wealth, the income from all this," he traced a wide arc in the air. "She has come home, where she belongs and where she is loved. You call this being in trouble?"

"She has always been loved, and she has never been in want." She saw a suspicious narrowing of the eyes at this, and wondered what on earth Allison might have told him about her upbringing. No doubt she had made it as pathetic and as dramatic as possible. "I believe she has no right to be here. There's no proof that she is your granddaughter, and I think she is being duped." She did not say it, but the implication was there, clear between them, that he was being duped as well.

"You are not afraid."

She couldn't tell from his tone whether that was a statement or a question, and so she left it unanswered. He seemed to shrink further back into the chair, as if the interview had already exhausted him.

"I am old," he said in a weary voice. "I will not have time to search further for my granddaughter even if it were necessary."

Was he actually admitting that she might be right, that Allison was very possibly a fraud? But when she opened her mouth to pursue this, he raised a hand to silence her.

"I am tired now, please go, Miss Conners. I extend to you the hospitality of my house, but I ask you to be a guest in it, not a source of further dissension. Now you will leave me. Ask Mrs. Brunner to come here, if you please."

"Surely." She turned and walked to the door, but before she had reached it his voice stopped her again.

"My son, Alex—he speaks highly of you," he said. It was not a remark that required an answer and she gave him none. "He is a fine boy," he murmured. "He has character."

His chin sank down upon his chest; whether he had fallen asleep or not she couldn't say. There were no further remarks to her, and she went out. Alex was gone, but Mrs. Brunner was just down the hall, obviously waiting.

"He asked to see you," Peggy said. Mrs. Brunner hurried off to the old man's room. Left alone in the hall, Peggy made her way downstairs to the parlor, where she expected to find Alex. Instead, she found herself face to face with Mrs. Marvel for the first time since she had arrived at the house.

The woman looked as eccentric as ever. She wore a knee-length smock over her dress and yet another wide-brimmed hat with a veil; she had evidently been outside working in a garden, for she wore gloves as well, and held a trowel in one hand.

"So, here you are," she said, smiling from behind

the veil. "Still trying to stir up your hornet's nest, I suppose."

"Trying to get at the truth would be more accurate. The truth that you know as well as I do."

"There are a great many things that I know that you do not know. The stars tell me many things, my dear."

"Just as they told you how to miraculously find Melissa?" Peggy could not entirely keep the sarcasm from her voice.

"It was the stars that guided her to me, and me to her. You scoff because you are ignorant, but the stars do not lie and they are never wrong. And that is why I know that it was foolish for you to come here, foolish and dangerous. This way lies humiliation, defeat, even tragedy. You follow a willful star, dear girl, willful and dangerous."

"And I suppose that you will connive to make that prediction come true, just as in your predictions about Melissa?"

Mrs. Marvel took an angry step closer and for a moment Peggy thought she meant to strike her with the trowel in her hand.

"Young fool, leave here at once, or you will have only yourself to blame for the consequences you will certainly suffer."

With that she whirled about and stalked from the room, leaving an ominous silence in her wake. Left alone, Peggy wondered where she would find Allison; perhaps another talk with her would do some good. And Alex too had disappeared.

When she went in to lunch a short time later she learned from Mrs. Brunner that Alex was working and had said he would not be back until evening. Allison was in her room; presumably, Peggy thought, avoiding me. Mrs. Marvel's instructions, no doubt.

Peggy spent a restless and nonproductive afternoon alone. She strolled about the house and the grounds, hoping without much conviction that she might yet run into Allison. Once she saw Alex in the vineyards and he waved, but she saw that he was busy and she didn't want to intrude. She even strolled down to the boathouse, but Waldo was there, polishing the fittings on the cruiser, and the look he gave her was anything but welcoming.

Finally, she settled in her room with a book from the library. So far, she reflected wryly, her coming here had accomplished nothing more than the stirring up of various personal animosities. Still, that might not be a bad thing. Allison seemed frightened of Mrs. Marvel and resentful of Alex. Jack hated Mrs. Marvel, and Alex had a not-very-flattering opinion of Jack. Well, if those dislikes and resentments were brought into the open, even encouraged a little, who could tell what truths might surface?

Mrs. Brunner had informed her that dinner was at seven, and shortly before that, dressed in the only really good dress she had brought with her, a long, dark blue velvet gown, she came down to the parlor. This time both Mrs. Marvel and Allison were there; the three of them were soon joined by Alex.

"Well, here we all are, one big happy family," Allison said. She was sipping a cocktail and, at Alex's invitation, Peggy had one as well.

"That's the closest you've come to admitting we're related," Peggy said archly.

Alex, having served the drinks, gave Allison a hard look. "Peggy says that when the two of you had your talk the other day, you finally admitted to being her stepsister."

"What of it?" Allison demanded petulantly. "That isn't the real question, is it? The point is that I am Melissa Gilbert. Of course I've lived a life in the intervening years since I was lost, but what difference does it make what that life was, now that I'm back?"

"Exactly," Mrs. Marvel said. "What can it matter then if she was Allison Someone-or-Other, or Mary Brown? She is now Melissa."

"But *is* she?" Alex persisted.

"We've been all through that before," Mrs. Marvel said impatiently.

"Yes, and I was convinced before, but now I'm just not so sure. All those things she knew, all the questions she answered—she could have been coached."

"That's nonsense," Allison said, putting her glass down on the table with a clunk. "In the first place, there wouldn't have been time to coach me in everything I remember. From the moment I stepped onto this island I remembered everything about it, just as if I'd never been away."

"There are many people who are familiar with the island," Alex said. "And with the family history. A good detective might have uncovered all the things you know; and a fast learner could have memorized much of it in a day or two."

Mrs. Marvel made a scoffing sound, but Allison only smiled confidently. To Peggy's surprise, Allison came close to Alex and put up one hand to toy playfully with the lapel of his jacket.

"And what detective do you think told me about the secret door in Grandfather's room—the door that leads to the basement, and from there, by a tunnel, to the wine buildings, and finally to the back gate itself? Do you think that is common knowledge too?"

Alex's face had grown pale as she spoke. He took her hand from his jacket and stared at her in amazement.

"No one knew of that door or the tunnel," he said, "no one but Father and I."

"So you thought," Allison said, laughing softly. "I discovered it as a little girl; Grandfather had the door open once when I came into his room, and I made him show me the tunnel in return for my promise never to tell anyone."

Peggy was once again aware of Mrs. Marvel. The woman had taken a step back and was staring at Allison with a surprise no less obvious than Alex's. She swayed slightly and put out a hand to the mantel to steady herself.

Alex suddenly turned toward her. "Did you know about the door and the tunnel?" he demanded.

Mrs. Marvel shook her head dazedly, as if she could not believe what she had heard. "No. I never heard of them till now." She turned slowly to face Allison. "But then . . . if I didn't tell you about that . . . then you really are . . ."

She did not finish. Allison's gleeful laugh silenced them all for a moment.

"I've got to have some time to think," Alex said. He started toward the French doors that led to the terrace.

Peggy ran after him and seized his sleeve. "Alex, this must be some sort of trick too. You don't believe it—do you?"

He stared down at her and for the moment at least she felt as if the two of them were again opponents. "I don't know just what I believe now," he said slowly. With that he was gone. She stood staring anxiously at the door through which he had disappeared.

Chapter 19

Alex did not return for dinner and Mrs. Marvel, seemingly stunned by Allison's revelation, decided that she would have something sent up to her room.

"I feel faint all of a sudden," she murmured, one hand at her breast.

Peggy and Allison went into the dining room alone. When they were seated, facing each other across the huge table, Peggy went back to the subject.

"Now that there're just the two of us," she said, "tell me, how did you know about that secret door and tunnel? And don't tell me you remembered it from your childhood."

"Look," Allison said, waving her fork like a weapon, "If I'm not going to be allowed to at least eat my dinner in peace, I'm going to have something sent up to my room too."

"Fair enough," Peggy agreed. She did not care for having a meal spoiled either; in any case, she thought she could get a lot more out of Allison in a relaxed mood. It was foolish to provoke her. "Let's have a truce till after dinner."

"That suits me fine," Allison said sulkily.

They ate more or less in silence, exchanging only a few desultory remarks on the dishes that Mrs. Brunner served in her heavy-handed manner. The food was good, solid German fare, heartier than Peggy was used to but quite acceptable.

Peggy's hopes for a more chatty Allison were dashed after dinner, however. Allison had no sooner finished her dessert than she pushed her chair back and announced that she thought she would retire early.

"I had hoped you and I would be able to talk a bit," Peggy said, reproaching her gently.

"What for?" Allison replied. "We've both said everything we have to say already. Good night."

Reluctantly Peggy watched her go. She had begun to believe that nothing she could say or do would get through to Allison. Allison had set her course for a distant—and dangerous—star, and nothing now could change her direction.

Peggy went in search of Alex instead. There was no sign of him in the parlor nor anywhere in the main downstairs rooms of the house. Thinking he might have gone to the office in the wine storage building, she left the house and followed the path in that direction.

That building was dark, though, and she could only conclude that he was in his room, or that he had left the estate. She started to walk down the drive that led to the boathouse, thinking to see if the boats were all there.

She had gotten only a few feet when she heard the sound of footsteps behind her. She turned, expecting to see Alex, and found herself confronting Jack instead.

"I saw you from my window," he said, pausing as though afraid she might bolt if he came too close.

164

"Since you were alone, I thought it would be a good time to come and talk to you."

"That will make you just about the only person in the place who wants to talk to me," she said peevishly. She hadn't yet worked off the black mood that Allison's stubbornness had effected.

"They're all fools," Jack said flatly. "Anyway, I'm the only one who might be able to help you."

Instantly she was alert. "What do you mean, help me?"

He smiled mysteriously. "Just that. I have something in my room that might make Melissa, or whoever she is, look foolish."

"What is it?" Peggy asked excitedly.

He wagged his finger at her. "Oh no, you don't get anything out of me that easily. First, you have to come up to my room to see it. I refuse to bring it down here and I refuse to tell you about it."

"You said 'first' I had to come to your room—what's the second thing?"

He gave a mischievous chuckle, but it sounded almost sinister in the moonlight. "Maybe I'll insist that you give me a kiss," he said.

She couldn't tell whether he was joking or not, but her determination to find some conclusive evidence against Allison's ruse was strong enough to withstand the price of a kiss.

"Where is your room?" she asked.

"This way." He took her arm, steering her toward the side door of the house.

She had thus far not ventured into this part of the house. Alex had told her that Jack had an apartment, or

165

suite of rooms, on the third floor, and now they took the back stairs, past the kitchen, and past the second floor. He paused at a door on the third floor.

"This is her room," he said in a tense whisper.

"Allison's?"

"No—that woman—Mrs. Marvel." He seemed frightened at the very thought of the woman, and gripped her arm in a viselike grip as he hurried on with her to the next door. He had to unlock it with a large brass key which he carried on a chain attached to his belt; apparently Jack valued his privacy very highly.

"This is my little domain," he said, ushering her in; she noted a bit apprehensively that he closed the door again behind them.

It was, she saw, an apartment complete in itself. Through one opened door she saw a small kitchenette, and through another she had a glimpse of a bedroom. He could live here within the house, and still not have to mix with the others at all.

"It's very nice," she said. Actually it had rather an old-maidish quality that she did not care for. But she saw something else: a lady's silk stocking hung over the shower curtain rod in the bathroom. Apparently— for all Jack's occasional prissiness—she was not the first lady guest he had had in his rooms of late.

"Would you like a drink?" he asked.

"I think not," Peggy said; she did not feel at all comfortable with him in this remote suite of rooms, especially now that his personal interest in her was no secret. "I'd rather see whatever it was you had to show me."

He went to a small bar and poured himself a drink. There was a tense, excited air about him, as if he were about to spring a surprise. "Well, it's right in front of you, if you'd only use your eyes," he said, stirring his drink with a silver spoon.

"I don't see . . . Oh." She had turned about to survey the room more carefully. On her first cursory glance she had passed over the portrait that hung above a velvet-covered settee. Now her eyes rested on it with surprise.

"That's her mother," Jack said, coming to stand just behind her. "Melissa's mother, I mean. It's the only picture of Claire around the place—I got Uncle Jacob to give it to me years ago, and by now I'm sure everyone's forgotten I have it."

She was uncomfortably aware of his nearness behind her and instinctively she took a step forward.

"If anything could trip her up," he went on, "it would be this. She claims she remembers everything now that she's come back to the island—but if she didn't recognize her—" he pointed dramatically toward the portrait—"it would prove conclusively she's a fake. Surely she would recognize her own mother, wouldn't she?"

"Yes, I would think so," Peggy said absent-mindedly. She was studying the portrait closely. Of course, part of the effect it had had came from a trick of the light, and the way the girl in the portrait wore her hair. And yet, on first sight it had seemed to her—no, it was impossible. Still, the girl in the painting was not at all unlike Allison.

"How old was she when this was painted?" she asked, staring again at the portrait.

"Twenty. It was just before she was married."

Almost Allison's age today, Peggy thought. Was it

possible after all that Allison was right? Of course, it was not an exact likeness; one could find countless pairs of girls, quite unrelated, who looked as much alike as Allison and the long-dead Claire—but there was enough of a resemblance to support the actuality that they were mother and daughter.

"Has Allison seen this?" she asked, wondering if Allison had deliberately styled herself after the portrait, to further the illusion.

"Of course not, I told you, this is how we can trip her up."

She couldn't share his enthusiasm. He had brought her here with a promise of something that would unmask Allison for a fraud; instead, he might very well have provided further evidence to support her claims.

Jack again moved closer and this time she felt the weight of his hands on her shoulders, turning her around to face him.

"Well, do I get my reward now?" he asked. The desire written on his face was impossible to misread. Yet for a moment there was something else there, as if he were hiding from her some private joke he'd made at her expense.

"Please, don't," she said, trying to twist free of his embrace. His face went ugly with anger—how mercurial his moods were.

"You promised," he said, not letting her go.

"No I didn't. Let me go, please." For a moment she actually had to struggle with him, and she was afraid that she had gotten herself in for a bad bargain. Then suddenly he released her, so unexpectedly that she nearly fell over the velvet settee. He was breathing hard and his voice was an angry rasp.

"You're just like all the others, aren't you?" he lashed out at her.

"I don't know what you mean by that," she said, "nor why you should expect a girl to submit just because you feel inclined to kiss her. A woman is a person too, you know, with her own feelings and ideas—and rights."

She turned and strode quickly to the door, half fearing that he would pursue her, or that the door would be locked. But he remained where he was, and the door opened easily at her touch.

"Good night," she said, glancing back. "And thank you for showing me the portrait."

He did not answer and she did not wait for him to decide to pursue his amorous inclinations. She hurried downstairs, going the same way they had come, by the back stairs. She wanted to go back outside, into the cool night air. Her face felt flushed. Above her, she heard a door open and close—Jack? Coming after her? She hurried on down the stairs and across the empty kitchen.

Outside she paused in the moonlight, breathing deeply, wanting to relax, to forget the pressure of Jack's fingers on her skin, the naked passion on his face as he moved his lips toward hers. She couldn't understand why he repulsed her so, why the thought of a kiss from him made her feel faintly ill.

She heard a voice—Alex's voice, coming from outside the house. She went in that direction, toward the side terrace. Briefly she heard another voice but it was too soft to distinguish. Then both voices stopped. Probably, she thought, they had gone back inside.

She came about the corner of the house and stopped

in her tracks, understanding at once why the voices had stopped so abruptly. Alex was still there and so was Allison, whose voice had been the second one she had heard. But neither of them was aware of her. At the moment they were too busy with each other—kissing.

Feeling heartsick, Peggy tried to turn away before they could discover her, but she was on gravel and a small crunching noise betrayed her. She heard a sharp, "What was that?"

She started to run, blindly, hardly knowing where she was going. Behind her she heard Alex cry, "Peggy, wait!" But she continued to run. Faintly, in the distance, she heard Allison's laugh—cruel, taunting.

Chapter 20

She had begun to run with no idea of where she was going, except that she wanted to get away from them; she could not bear to see the expression on Alex's face, be it guilty or indifferent.

She found after a moment that her feet had carried her in the direction of the boathouse, and soon looming over her were the gates and the stone lions. Did they look down upon her now with scorn and disdain as she ran beneath them—those cruel beasts that knew the answers to all her questions, if only they would speak?

But their words, if they spoke, would be words of warning: *Beware, we stand at the gates of hell.* And perhaps there was truth to that after all.

The small outboard motorboat was tied up at the dock. Hardly thinking what she was doing, she cast off and leaped inside. She yanked the starter rope and the motor leaped to life and she moved in reverse away from the dock. She heard someone yell—it sounded unlike Alex's voice this time, but on the water it was sometimes difficult to tell.

She put the boat into forward and opened the throttle. The noise racketed in the air as she gained speed.

She really had no idea where she was going—not into shore, certainly. What she needed now was to be alone, and she wanted the sensation of speed and wind and spray and the shield of darkness. Already it was beginning to calm her and she let up a bit on the throttle, steering out toward the open water. There were no other boats around at this time of night; the tourists had returned to shore, to their hotels and motels, the fishermen were waiting for the dawn. Overhead she heard the whine of a jet winging swiftly on its way to some distant place.

Allison and Alex. Allison and Melissa. Melissa and Jack. Jack and Claire. Claire and old Jacob Lions. And Mrs. Marvel, always the evil alter ego, standing in the shadows, manipulating.

Perhaps they had all been right, perhaps she should never have come. Perhaps she should leave now. She had faced Allison and said what she had to say, and Allison had revealed to her a side of her nature that Peggy had never known existed—cruel instead of merely willful. Right now Allison was living an illusion; but for all these years, Peggy had loved an illusion too, an impression that she had had of Allison that was only part of the truth, and not even the major part at that.

There was another boat out there; she could hear the roar of a powerful engine in the distance. She looked over her shoulder and saw a spotlight sweeping across the water—someone was searching for something.

Someone searching for me? she thought with a sudden tingling of fear. She listened again—a big boat, bigger and far more powerful than this one; a cruiser—

like the one in the boathouse at Lions Island. The spotlight moved over the water, left, then right, then left.

"It's probably Alex, feeling guilty, wanting to apologize to me," she told herself. At almost the same moment she flipped the switch, cutting off the running lights on the outboard. She cut back the throttle too, to lessen the noise of her boat, and listened.

It was coming closer, the powerful beam of light inching nearer and nearer to her. In a moment or two it would reveal her boat.

Gradually, hoping not to attract attention to herself, she pushed the throttle forward and at the same time cut the wheel sharply to the right, toward the darkness that lay that side of the beam's sweep.

There was, however, no way to accelerate quietly in an outboard. The sound of her motor was like a shout in the night. She saw the beam of light stop in midsweep and arc back toward her.

Instinct took over. An inner voice told her that that light was bringing no safety, no good intentions. It was like a threatening finger pointing at her in the darkness.

She thrust the throttle full forward. The boat hesitated for a moment, then surged ahead, nose lifting. The water was choppy this far out and her small boat bounced and slammed against the water, rocking, bucking. She turned wide, hoping to throw off pursuit, but the cruiser behind her, its own engine now ascending in pitch as it accelerated, was too fast. Halfway through her turn the light caught her. She sat trapped in its blinding glare, her mouth open in a little gasp of fright.

It was coming full down upon her, its speed still increasing, the light holding her like a butterfly beneath a pin.

They were going to ram her!

She grabbed the wheel and pulled hard to the right, flinging herself against the side of the boat. It veered, threatening to flip over, but it turned, seemingly into the path of the cruiser, while the turn carried her just to the side. The cruiser rushed past her, its wake flinging her about like a cork in a bucket.

She leaned forward against the dash, limp with fear. She was drenched and there was water ankle high in the bottom of the outboard, but she was still afloat, and the cruiser, for all its power, wasn't maneuverable enough to spin around on a dime. It was slowing, turning to come back, but its turn was a wide, lazy-seeming one.

She pushed the throttle again and cried out in frustration. The motor had stalled. Hands trembling, she pushed the starter. It sputtered and coughed and finally died again.

She crawled to the back, agonizingly aware of the water in the bottom of the boat—water that would slow her down, maybe even swamp her eventually. If this one was like the engine on their boat at home—it was. A little hatch lifted in the front of the motor housing, and there were the controls for the automatic choke. She flipped it off and crawled forward again.

This time the engine caught. She looked back and saw a giant eye of light staring through the night directly at her.

She opened it flat out, heading not for Lions Island but for where she guessed the nearest inhabited island to be, somewhere off to her left. The boat shook and bucked beneath her. She prayed that there were no obstructions in the water, floating logs or other debris that she would miss without her running lights, the sort of thing that could send the boat hurtling into the air, end over end . . .

She looked back and knew she would never make it; already the cruiser had cut the distance between them in half and it was gaining rapidly. The spotlight's beam was trailing the water just a few feet behind her.

She no longer had any hope that this was a friendly search for her. Whoever was piloting that cruiser intended to kill her. But who could it be—Waldo? Mrs. Marvel? Jack?

The obvious answer was Alex. It was he who had seen her, who had run after her, calling her name. But why—why should he want to kill her? Had she trusted the wrong one after all? Had his sweetness, his romancing, his kindness, only been another move on their part to throw her off the scent?

The light caught her, hesitated, then struck her full in the back, casting her shadow eerily over the dashboard of the boat. Her own boat seemed to vibrate with the power of the cruiser's motor. It loomed like an awful monster behind her.

Again she pulled frantically on the wheel, to the left, then back to the right, cutting a zigzag course. The little boat was more agile than the cruiser; it was her only chance, the only possibility she had for escape.

The cruiser stayed with her, picking up speed; incredibly, it still had power in reserve. It was a nightmarish cat and mouse game over the surface of the choppy water, and she was losing.

She knew she could never make the island now.

Somewhere far off to the right she saw the running lights of another boat. If she could get close enough, so that they could see what was happening—surely whoever was in the cruiser would not kill her in front of eyewitnesses. And if her boat was swamped, there might be someone to rescue her from the water—if she was alive.

She swung hard to the right. For a second she lost them, the cruiser making a far wider and slower turn. But it was a turn that again brought them after her at an angle—an angle, she realized with a sinking in the bottom of her stomach, that would intersect her line of flight.

The light was on her left now, zooming down upon her like an avenging angel. She had to make another turn, away from that distant boat that might mean safety.

And once again, her engine stalled.

The cruiser roared past, slowing abruptly to turn back. Her legs barely supported her as she crawled back to the engine. She flipped the choke back, and clambered frantically back to the controls.

The engine wouldn't start. It sputtered and whined and refused to come to life. She heard the cruiser's engine slow as it made its turn, then gradually begin to grow louder. They were coming back, again coming at a line that would strike her alongside, and they were coming fast, flat-out now. The chase was over.

She cried in frustration, holding her thumb glued to the starter button.

Nothing.

The light struck her full-face as she turned to look at it in terror. For a second or two more she hesitated. Then she leapt up, scrambling for a foothold on the vinyl seat—and dived into the water in front of the cruiser, directly in its path.

Chapter 21

Impossible to tell how deep she had dived, how far
she had swum. If she came up under the boat or worse,
into its engine . . . She exhaled all the air from her
lungs, diving deep, and swam with all the strength she
had, down and forward at the same time, trying to swim
under the length of the boat and come up behind it. But
her lungs constricted in pain; they ached for air and her
limbs already felt weighted with iron.

Finally she could go no further, she had to breathe.
She shot upward, searching for the surface. She broke it
at last, coughing, choking on lake water and gasping
for air. Her eyes opened on the blackness of the night,
with stars shining innocently above. Her arms still
flailed at the black weight of the water and her legs
kicked wildly. For a moment she was out of control;
she sank again. The cold water brought her back to her
senses.

The lake, the cruiser in that horrible pursuit, the final
crash even as she had dived. She surfaced again, shaking the water from her eyes, and looked.

She could see nothing of the outboard—it must have
splintered at once from the impact. But there, further

away than she would have expected, was the cruiser, not moving now, the engine down to an idle.

She trod water, grateful to feel a shoe slip from her foot. Her clothes were weighting her down and, treading water clumsily, she managed to get out of the dress and the other shoe. Then she looked again.

Darkness, and there to her left, some yards away, the cruiser, with its spotlight again sweeping the water, but just now in the opposite direction.

They would look for her, of course—whoever it was in the cruiser; they would want to make very sure that they'd been successful. The only thing she could really hope for was that they would give up eventually, conclude that she was dead, and go back to the island.

The engine increased in sound and the cruiser began to move slowly, searching the water. At the moment it was moving away at an angle, but she knew it would swing back this way at any moment. She began to swim. She wasn't sure just how far it was to one of the islands, or even how far she could swim. A mile perhaps—she was a moderately good swimmer. But what if she were swimming in the wrong direction? She might be swimming toward Canada, right out into the middle of that huge lake.

She lost track of the cruiser. Perhaps they had cut their lights now, thinking to see her better by moonlight. The waves were just ample enough to get lost in their troughs. Her arms and legs ached and she already had begun to wonder if she could go much further. And still there was no sight of land.

Gasping for breath, she stopped to tread water, to try to rest a moment—and she caught the scent of gasoline in the wind, and saw a hundred yards or so away the running lights of a boat. The cruiser? She had no way of knowing now, and she dared not shout for help, lest it bring the wrong person.

She could hear the engine throbbing now, coming closer. And then the spotlight again, scanning the water, back and forth.

She dived, down again into that inky, cold blackness, praying to heaven and to the ancient sea gods, to any ears that would listen.

When she came up, the boat had gone, she could no longer hear the muffled roar of its engine. And as a wave—perhaps a remnant of the cruiser's wake—lifted her for a moment, she saw trees in the distance. An island. She began to swim desperately in that direction.

Five minutes later, treading water to sight the island's trees again, she knew she would never reach it. Her arms were so leaden she could barely lift them to stroke the water, and for all she could tell a shark might have bitten off her legs; they were completely numb. She could barely keep herself afloat, and after a moment she couldn't even do that, she was sinking into the water, carried down as on the wings of a sea god, some mythical creature of the deep, bearing her down to a place where there was golden light and music and sweet perfume—how foolish to struggle on when she need only close her eyes, give herself up to the dream that was enveloping her. In a moment she would open her eyes again and it would be morning, and Alex would be there, calling her name . . .

He was already there. She heard his voice as from afar: "Peggy. Peggy."

She was on the surface, some instinct keeping her limbs moving, and there was the voice, calling, calling . . . But this was no dream, it was real, that was Alex's voice, and the boat was back, close now, and the light . . .

"Alex!" It was like a gasp, a murmur, carried away on the winds, over the lake, over the woods, far away to lands where men had never dwelt. "Alex."

And finally, she could do no more, could care no more, the dream was too insistent, too comforting, and she closed her eyes and drifted into the waiting darkness.

She awakened to the pain of retching and coughing, and the realization that she was lying on the rough floor of a boat.

"Easy, there, easy, it's all right now," a voice was saying. She opened her eyes and found herself looking up into Alex's concerned face.

"Alex, oh, Alex," she tried to say, but what came out was a fresh burst of retching.

It was a long while before she was able to sit up. Alex took off his coat and wrapped it around her and bundled her into the seat beside him. Then he headed the boat for home.

"How—how did you find me?" she managed to ask finally, when the shivering had lessened a bit.

"I came after you right away, but I didn't realize you had gone to the boathouse until I heard motors starting up. Then I came out in this one to look for you, and I saw all sorts of crazy goings on with the lights, someone searching the water—I thought you were overboard, so I headed this way, but then the lights disappeared, and the boat got away from me—what happened, anyway?"

"Someone chased me, tried to swamp me. They rammed the outboard, and I dived into the water. I was trying to swim to an island."

He turned to look into her face and she saw a cold anger in his eyes. "Who did it?" he asked in a low, icy voice.

She shook her head. "I couldn't see. I thought . . ." She checked herself, but not quickly enough.

"You thought it was me?" When she didn't answer, he said, "My God."

They didn't talk after that until they reached Lions Island. Alex tied up the boat at the landing and helped her out. She felt weak but she was able to stand and walk.

He went straight to the boathouse, Peggy at his heels.

There was no doubt that this had been the cruiser chasing her. It wore the scars of the battle. The nose was gouged and splintered, and one plank along the side had separated from another at the water line. It was still afloat, but whoever had been piloting it had given up the search for her not out of conviction that she was dead, but clearly because he had had to limp home with this boat before it too sank.

But there was nothing, unfortunately, to tell her who had been piloting the cruiser.

He took her arm to steady her and together they walked toward the house. They saw no one on the way, nor when they came into the house. It lay still about them, everyone seemingly abed for the night.

"Very cozy," he said. "Come on, you want some brandy to warm you up and a hot bath, then to bed. I'll straighten all this out in the morning."

She did not argue but let him take charge of the

situation. He poured the brandy, and while she sipped it in her bedroom, he filled a hot tub for her.

"Okay, in there," he told her when it was ready, "and then straight to bed. And lock your door tonight, as soon as I go out. Don't worry, I'll be asleep across the hall."

"Do you think someone might. . . ?"

"I don't know, but there's no point in taking chances. And there's one other thing—I had no idea what I was letting you in for when I brought you out here, but now that I do know, I won't allow it to continue. In the morning, you're moving back to the mainland."

She could not help a small feeling of disappointment; she had come with such high hopes, and aside from antagonizing everyone and almost getting herself killed, she had accomplished nothing. But just now she hadn't the strength nor the will to oppose his command. She nodded mutely and went to soak in the tub.

Chapter 22

Alex was waiting for her when she came down in the morning. Except for a slight cough and some soreness in her overexercised muscles, she did not feel too bad for last night's misadventure. She was regretting, however, Alex's decision that she must leave this morning. Suddenly confident in his feeling for her, she felt less threatened than she had before the incident.

"You all right this morning?" he asked her when he'd greeted her.

"Yes. Did you—talk to the others?"

"Yes, but no one knows anything about the boat. According to their stories they were each in their rooms, unaware anything was happening."

"Well, there's one thing I know for certain, someone was in that boat. Someone who wanted me dead."

"There's one other thing you ought to know," he said, looking down at his shoes. "Last night, when you saw Allison and me . . ."

"It's really none of my business," she said quickly.

"But it is. I want you to know. It was just, I was outside looking for you and she came out. She was teasing, I suppose, or trying to get close to me because she sensed I still wasn't sure—or maybe she realized how I felt about you and was just jealous. I'm not excusing myself, understand—I didn't have to let her do that. I'm just saying it didn't mean anything.''

"I understand," Peggy said. Actually, she had heard very little after he had said "how I felt about you . . ."

"I just wanted you to know how it was," he said, searching her eyes for some sign. But then, impulsively, he closed the space between them and his arms went about her. He kissed her, and she knew that nothing else mattered—none of this foolishness with Allison, not even the danger she had been in last night, nothing mattered but that out of it she had found this man whom she loved as she had never dreamed it was possible to love.

The gods had decreed that her happiness be short-lived, however, The kiss ended soon, too soon, and after a dreamy moment she was aware that someone else had come into the room.

She looked over her shoulder to see Allison there. At that moment she was glad to have Allison see them like this, to learn for herself that her childish prank of the night before was of no consequence. But then Peggy became aware that the look on Allison's face signified something more than anger or jealousy, it was a look of stunned horror.

"Allison, what is it, what's wrong," she asked, freeing herself from Alex's embrace and going to her sister. For once Allison welcomed the comfort of her arms.

"It's Grandfather," she said, sagging weakly against Peggy. "He . . . he's dead."

Jacob Lions had indeed passed on. He had succumbed at last to the years and to the illness that had been ravaging him so relentlessly. Peggy was saddened by his going, and saddened too that it put a wall of grief between her and Alex just when they had resolved everything between each other.

But in a sense she was glad that Jacob Lions had died with his illusions regarding Melissa intact. He had believed to the end that his beloved granddaughter had come home to him.

This change in the situation now brought home to Peggy more urgently than ever that Allison was now in grave danger from her fellow conspirators. And regardless of the way Allison had treated her of late, she could not just abandon her.

She found Allison in her room. To her surprise, Allison seemed genuinely grieved by Jacob Lions' death. She was pale and drawn-looking and she was smoking nervously. The ashtray by her bed was filled to overflowing.

"Allison," Peggy said, closing the door after herself and coming across to the bed where Allison was stretched out.

Allison turned red-rimmed eyes toward her. "How many times do I have to tell you, the name is Melissa."

"Allison, Melissa—it doesn't matter anymore. What does matter is that the old man's death changes everything for you. Surely you can see that."

Allison smiled, a strange, bittersweet smile. "You're right, darling, it does change everything. It was one thing to go along with that old witch's schemes in order to get back here, and while I was here to get myself squared away with Grandfather. But none of that matters anymore, as you say. He's gone now, and I am the heir.''

Her face was positively triumphant. ''I own all this now, Peggy. Not Mrs. Marvel, or Alex, or Jack—just me.''

Peggy stared at her in horror. ''And you mean to tell them that? You mean to turn your back on Mrs. Marvel?''

''There's nothing she can do.'' Allison blew another cloud of smoke into the already smoke-filled room. ''Once the will's probated, it'll be mine, completely mine.''

Peggy sat on the edge of the bed and clasped one of Allison's hands in her own. ''Then it's more important than ever that you come away from here. Leave it to Alex or Jack or the authorities to get rid of Mrs. Marvel and Waldo. Don't you see, Mrs. Marvel has schemed all these years for this, she won't let you just snatch it all out of her hands. I don't know what she'll do, but my guess is that the minute she hears of your intentions, your life is going to be in grave danger!''

Allison puffed thoughtfully for a few minutes. ''You may be right,'' she said finally.

''I know I am. Look, it doesn't matter what's happened between you and me—you don't even have to come home with me. Just leave with me, and go somewhere, anywhere, until she's out of here and the will has been probated.'' At the moment Peggy did not even care whether or not Allison thought she truly believed she was Melissa; just now she was thinking only of Allison's safety.

Allison gave her a grateful look for the first time

since she had disappeared from Hunter's Point. "It's sweet of you to worry about me, really, Peg, I know I have been a pill lately. Look, don't worry, I'll tell you what, I'll come to the hotel tonight. I won't come back to Columbus with you—that part of my life is finished —but I'll leave with you tonight and we can go someplace, till I can get settled in."

Peggy patted her hand affectionately. "I'm glad you see it that way," she said. "And remember, don't say anything to Mrs. Marvel about what you've planned."

"Don't worry, *she* won't stop me." It was not exactly the promise Peggy had wanted, but she did not want to risk Allison's friendlier mood by pressing her for more.

"Till tonight then," she said, standing again.

Allison flashed a smile that Peggy thought was a little too bright, a little too tense. But she smiled back and let herself out of the room.

She found Alex in the hall looking for her. His face looked lined and weary, but he took her warmly in his arms.

"Look," he said, "I've got to go into town. There're the authorities to see, and Father's lawyers to contact—not to mention business affairs that will need taking care of. And I don't want to leave you here on your own. How soon can you get your things together?"

"It'll only take me a few minutes," Peggy said. Now that she had persuaded Allison to come away from here, she did not regret leaving Lions Island—and Alex would be too busy over the next day or so to have time for her.

"Good. I'll meet you in the parlor," he said.

It was less than half an hour later that she came down to the parlor, but it was Jack, not Alex, who was sitting there. He rose when she came in and greeted her as warmly as if there had been no quarrel between them the night before.

"You're not leaving," he exclaimed, catching sight of the case she was carrying.

"Yes, I think I'll be more comfortable in town," she said smoothly.

"But there's no need to dash away, just because Uncle Jacob passed on. He'd want you to stay, I know. And you needn't worry about Mrs. Marvel; she's ill today—too much night air, I suppose."

There was a malicious glint of amusement in his eyes, as if he knew something secret and wicked. She wondered if he was hinting that Mrs. Marvel had been the one in the boat the night before.

"What do you mean, 'too much night air'?" she asked. "Was she out on the lake last night?"

Jack shrugged and chuckled. "She wouldn't like me to tell everything I know. Besides, you didn't reward me properly the last time I shared one of my secrets with you."

He put a hand on her arm. Despite herself she felt the same revulsion she'd felt last night when he had tried to kiss her. But she forced herself not to pull her arm away.

"Do you know who tried to kill me last night?" she asked, looking boldly into his eyes.

"I know who tried to kiss you," he parried with a maddening snicker.

"And I know who's going to lose his teeth if he tries

it again,'' Alex said, choosing that inopportune moment to come into the room.

Jack, looking genuinely frightened, yanked his hand from Peggy and backed away from her. ''I was only being friendly,'' he whined. ''You should be grateful; *I'm* the only one who's tried to make her welcome here.''

He did not wait for a reply but hurried from the room. Peggy didn't know whether to be pleased by Alex's display of jealousy or annoyed that he might have interrupted an important bit of news. In any case, the damage was done.

''I'll just be a few minutes more,'' Alex said. ''Sorry to keep you waiting, but I've got a couple more phone calls that have to be made.''

''I don't mind,'' Peggy said. ''I'll meet you down by the boat.''

He kissed her and went out of the room. When he was gone, though, her thoughts went back to Mrs. Marvel and to Jack's veiled hints regarding her. Could it have been Mrs. Marvel in the cruiser last night? The woman had an air of frailty about her but she was actually a big woman, strong enough to handle a boat like a man. Jack had said she was sick today; perhaps this was the perfect time to visit her. It might be that, feeling under the weather, she would be less on her guard than before.

Jack had pointed out Mrs. Marvel's room to her last night and now she went to the third floor and knocked on that door. There was a brief silence and then a strained voice asked, ''Who is it?''

''It's Peggy.''

"What do you want?" the voice asked.

"Jack said you were ill, I thought I'd look in on you. May I come in?"

There was another pause and then, "Wait just a moment."

Peggy waited in silence. There were sounds from inside that she couldn't identify, and the creak of a floorboard as someone crossed a room. Then, just when she was beginning to think Mrs. Marvel wouldn't see her, the voice called, "You can come in now."

The room was as dark as night; only the light that spilled in from the hall, and a faint glow from the heavily curtained windows, made it possible for Peggy to make out heavy furniture.

"What do you want?" Mrs. Marvel's familiar voice asked from the bed.

Peggy came closer, but even standing by the bed she was barely able to distinguish the figure sitting up in it, let alone observe her expression.

"I just wanted to see how you were feeling," Peggy said. "Would you like me to turn on a light?" She reached for the switch but Mrs. Marvel stopped her with a harsh "No! I have a headache. The light makes it worse."

"Oh, I see, I'm sorry."

There was a long and awkward silence. It was Mrs. Marvel who finally broke it. "Mrs. Brunner tells me the old man is dead."

"Yes."

"I saw that in the stars as well. I knew his time had come. And yours has come too. There's nothing more to keep you here."

"I'm going," Peggy said. "I'm leaving in a few minutes."

She sensed that this time she had succeeded in surprising the woman in the bed. There was a creaking of springs and a rustling of the bedclothes that she held up to her chin.

"No one told me of this," she said sharply.

"I saw no reason to make an announcement of it," Peggy said with a shrug.

"Well, I must say I'm glad. You were foolish to come here in the first place, as I told you before. There was nothing you could do—then or now."

"Perhaps." There was another weighty silence; this time Mrs. Marvel did not break it, and feeling that she was getting nowhere, Peggy decided to go.

"I just wanted to wish you well," she said, turning toward the door. "Good-bye."

"You're leaving now? Leaving the estate, I mean?"

"Yes."

"Good-bye then."

Peggy went out. As she closed the door, she heard the sounds of the woman clambering out of bed. Apparently her news had cured Mrs. Marvel's indisposition. She wondered who or what she was hurrying off to see—Allison? Waldo? Jack? Even with the hatred between them, she and Jack were two of a kind, more alike than either of them would be willing to admit.

But, at least, she told herself, hurrying to the boat landing to meet Alex, I'm out of it all now, whatever happens.

Peggy had no way of knowing how mistaken she was.

Chapter 23

Alex was in agreement with Peggy's efforts to get Allison out of the house. "If she was in collusion with Mrs. Marvel, and plans on ditching her now, she'd be a fool to stay around there until Mrs. Marvel is gone," he said. "That woman is capable of just about anything."

"She said she'd see me tonight. I don't know what exactly she'll agree to, but if we leave town I'll let you know where we are," Peggy said.

"Fine. I'll be pretty tied up the next day or two anyway. Just make sure you don't stay lost."

"Small chance," she said, laughing.

They parted at the town landing, with her insistence that there was no need for him to see her to the hotel. She watched him go until the boat had dwindled to a spot in the distance. Then she strolled nonchalantly back to the hotel. Mrs. Roberts had promised to save her room for her and soon Peggy was once again comfortably installed there.

After lunch, she put in a call to Columbus. She did not give her mother the full story of everything that had happened, but she assured her that Allison was all right.

"And she looks in the way of becoming an heiress," Peggy added.

"It all sounds very mysterious," her mother said. "And how about you, anyway, are you all right? you sound like you've got a cold."

"I'm fine, really, I got a little wet last night," Peggy said, smiling into the receiver. There was no point in upsetting her parents by telling them what actually had happened to her. In any case, that was history now; with Jacob Lions dead, and Allison preparing to leave the island, Peggy regarded her part in the drama as ended; she was certainly not in any further danger, as no one now had any reason to want to be rid of her.

She spent a lazy afternoon strolling about the town; she was more relaxed than she had been since she arrived here, and for the first time could actually enjoy the resort town atmosphere. As evening approached, she had an early dinner and went back to her room to wait for Allison.

It was shortly before eight when Allison called. "I'm in the lobby," she said, sounding breathless and uncertain. "I wanted to be sure you were there before I came up."

"No problems getting away?"

There was a pause. "I don't think so. I thought I saw . . . well, we can talk when I come up."

Peggy hung up and waited, glancing every few seconds toward the door. Something about the tone of Allison's voice had brought back her former uneasiness. Allison had sounded—frightened. For the first time since she had gotten herself into this situation, Peggy wondered if Mrs. Marvel had somehow learned that Allison was planning to leave. It would have been just like Allison to tell her so herself, to taunt her with the news.

"Oh, Allison, how do you get yourself into these things," Peggy asked silently. She glanced at her watch. How long had it been since Allison had called—two, three minutes? Surely she had time to reach the room by now.

Peggy waited, and as she waited she began to grow increasingly tense, her glance going more and more often to the door. But no knock came, and when she looked at her watch again, she saw that nearly another four minutes had gone by.

"She couldn't have forgotten the room number, since she just called me," Peggy reasoned with herself. What else could have happened—unless an elevator was stuck, there was hardly any reason why it should take close to ten minutes to come from the lobby up to a room.

She waited another two minutes. Then, grabbing her purse from atop the dresser, she left the room and hurried down to the lobby.

There was no sign of Allison, not in the lobby, not in the restaurant's coffee shop. She saw the house phone on a wall, from which Allison must have phoned the room—but no Allison.

Mrs. Roberts herself was at the front desk, but she was not very helpful. "Yes, I think I remember a girl who looked like that," she said. "Strikingly pretty."

"Did you see what happened to her?" Peggy asked.

Mrs. Roberts screwed up her face thoughtfully, taking a moment to push back the glasses that had slipped down on her nose.

"No, I can't rightfully say I did. I have a vague

impression she left with some people—no, with a man. No, it was two people, a man and a woman. I think. But I can't be certain."

"Can you say what they looked like, or which way they went?"

Mrs. Roberts shook her head apologetically. "Really, I'm afraid I'm not being very helpful, but I just didn't notice. I'm not even sure we're talking about the same girl. You know how it is, so many people come in and out of here every day . . ." She sighed and shrugged.

"Well, thanks anyway," Peggy said bleakly. She walked out to the sidewalk, looking up and down as if she expected to find Allison waiting there for her. A man walking his dog gave her an appreciative glance but just now she was too worried to be flattered.

Could it have been Mrs. Marvel and Waldo that the hotelkeeper saw with Allison? If it was Allison. They might have learned her plans, perhaps from Allison herself. And they could have followed her here, persuaded her to come with them by threatening a scene, or with some other argument. But would Allison have gone, without calling back to say she had been delayed? It was hard to say; in the last few days Peggy had discovered she hardly knew Allison at all. A week ago she would have been sure Allison could not get herself mixed up in a drama as devilish as this.

She hesitated for a moment more outside the hotel; then, deciding that anything was preferable to indecision, she began to walk toward the boat landing. If Allison was not at the hotel, the only logical explanation was that for some reason she had gone back to Lions Island.

"And if the mountain won't come to Mohammed," Peggy thought drily, "Mohammed must come to the mountain."

Once again she found herself approaching the island by night, alone; this time she did not attempt to steal into the place. For one thing, she had no reason to think she would not be allowed to enter freely. Allison had disappeared, true, but Allison had disappeared before, without a word of explanation.

She tied up the boat, rented from old George again and started toward the house. But this time she found that the Lions' gate was closed, and locked.

After a moment's hesitation, she rang the bell. She waited what seemed an interminable time and was about to ring it again when she saw Mrs. Brunner trudging along the driveway toward the gates.

"I'm sorry, miss, I have instructions that no visitors are to be permitted," she said, stopping on the other side of the wrought-iron gate.

"I see," Peggy said. "I wonder, is my . . . is Melissa here?"

"She left, some time ago."

"Do you know where she went?"

"I couldn't say," was the ambiguous answer. Mrs. Brunner looked disinterested and impatient to get about her own business. She had almost turned to go back when Peggy stopped her again.

"Is Mr. Alex here, then? I'd like to see him if I may."

"He's not here either. He went to Cleveland, to see the lawyers." She paused and then added, "Said he wouldn't be back until tomorrow."

Mrs. Brunner did not wait to be questioned further but strode up the driveway toward the house. In a moment she was out of sight around the curve, not even acknowledging Peggy's feeble, "Thank you."

Tomorrow. Alex was gone until tomorrow. And if Allison were in some further trouble, tomorrow might be too late.

Peggy walked thoughtfully back to the dock where she had tied up the rented boat. Really, it was no longer any of her business. Allison had made it clear, not once but repeatedly, that she no longer considered what she did anyone's business but her own. Allison would say, "Go your own way, stop worrying about me."

But I can't stop worrying, Peggy thought, arguing silently, with Allison, with herself. *You have been my sister for fourteen years, and in my mind, if not in yours, you still are.*

It might be nothing more than a mistake, after all. Allison might have forgotten something she had to do; or she might have changed her mind. She might have decided that, while she did want to leave the island, she didn't want to leave with Peggy. She had said she did not want to go to Columbus, home to the family; maybe she had decided that Peggy represented too much of that past she wanted to be done with.

Then why did she call from the lobby? Why bother to come to the hotel at all?

All right, suppose—just suppose—that Allison was in further trouble. Suppose Mrs. Marvel had made her come back to the house, to iron out their future plans. Suppose that she wouldn't let Allison leave at all.

What does that matter to me? Allison told me to leave her alone. Whatever she's into, she got into it herself, on her own. It was an agony to me, too, worrying about her, hunting her, and then being rejected.

Which of course was sheer nonsense, the hurt of rejection was nothing compared to being in actual danger; and if Allison was brought back here against her will, was being somehow kept prisoner here, she was in deadly danger.

And she did owe Allison something, in the same way that Alex owed her something, and she owed Mother and Father something, and so on through that whole complicated structure that men and women had built and named civilization. Because, she thought, inevitably, no matter how we might want to rationalize our way out of troublesome situations, we are in at least some measure our brothers' keepers. Because we were all members of the club called the human race, and we have dues to pay as members, and because there are all those acts of kindness and concern others have done for us, and it is sometimes necessary to balance the ledger sheet.

She cast off the lines and jumped into the boat, starting the engine up. She steered toward the shore, wondering if by chance anyone on the island were watching her departure. Probably.

When she was far enough away that she knew she would not be seen in the darkness, she switched off the running lights, and turned around, heading back, around the island, to the place she had tied up on her first clandestine visit to the island.

Chapter 24

It was easier this second time finding her way in, tying the boat up to the rocks, wading through the surf. She had worn a skirt, but it was simple enough to remove her shoes and tie her skirt up under her belt until she was on the rocky beach. She stood for a moment getting her bearings. Then she began to follow along the stone wall, looking for the forgotten door that led inside.

She found it. It was still unlocked, and she slipped inside, pausing again, this time to listen. There were no signs or sounds of activity down this way, and she began to move stealthily along the path. This time at least she knew her way about the grounds, was familiar with the house, knew where the back entrance was. It would be fairly simple to get inside—provided no one saw her.

No one did between the gate and the house. At last she crept across the back lawn; there were the steps leading up to the kitchen door. There were lights at the kitchen window and she stood in the shadows of a tree for a few minutes, watching; she saw no one moving inside.

She decided not to chance that room, and went around the house to the side terrace. The parlor was dark, and the French doors unlocked. She hesitated then pushed the door open and stepped inside.

She was immediately enveloped by a sense of danger, as if she had stepped over the threshold into another world, frought with shadows and eerie silence. The quiet around her was intense, as if her stealthy entrance had made the house hush and hold its breath, waiting to see what she would do next. The house seemed to have a life and being all its own. The House of Lions seemed alive.

She stood very still near the fireplace and listened carefully. The silence seemed to smother her. The scent of a recent fire came to her, and a faint trace of some sickeningly sweet perfume—had that been Allison's?

But she could not remain where she was, listening, waiting for a dreaded footstep in the hall. Her courage seemed to have failed her. She realized that if anything went wrong, if she were attacked, or found here, there would be no one to hear her scream, no one to come to her rescue.

Stop being silly, she ordered herself. She crossed the parlor to the hall. There were no lights on here either but the lights from the kitchen and one from upstairs fell into the hall, casting a faint glow. She went on cat's feet toward the kitchen. Again she had the eerie feeling that the house had a living spirit all its own. For all the silence about her, she felt a presence of evil.

She reached the open door to the kitchen and still she had seen or heard nothing except for the creak of a floorboard beneath her foot.

There was no one in the kitchen, but across the room

the door to the basement stood open. Were they down there? She was about to cross the kitchen to that door when she heard a sound behind her, and whirled about. Someone was descending the main stairs. There was no escape by that route and she darted into the kitchen, pressing herself into the niche created by the refrigerator and the wall next to it.

She had a glimpse of Mrs. Brunner entering the kitchen. She went to the cellar stairs and called down, "There's a boat coming."

Waldo and Mrs. Marvel appeared at the top of the cellar stairs. Fortunately none of them looked in her direction; they were all in a hurry to get upstairs where they would have a view of the lake.

She waited until they disappeared down the hall. Then, holding her breath, she dashed for the basement door, and down the steps.

It was musty and dim down here, and a spider's web brushed her arm, almost making her cry out. She paused near the bottom, trying to accustom her eyes to the gloom.

This was the family's private wine cellar. The racks stretched back into the shadows, filled with bottles of wine, the best of their vintages and no doubt great wines from around the world as well.

There was not a sound from down here; apparently the basement was empty. Was she on a wild goose chase? What if Allison were not here at all? What if this very moment Allison were waiting at her hotel, wondering what had happened to her?

She was almost convinced to leave, to hurry back to the boat, and to town, to see if Allison were really there.

And then she saw the bricks—piles of them, and a barrow full of mortar. And beyond them, a half finished wall.

They had been walling off one end of the room. Surely an odd occupation for that crew, in the middle of the night—unless . . .

Oh God, she didn't even want to think it. She moved with leaden limbs down the remaining few steps, across the narrow width of the wine cellar to the newly constructed wall of bricks. It was almost waist high by now, half finished—a pretty night's work.

She reached the wall, leaned forward to look in—and sucked in her breath.

Allison was there, lying in a crumpled heap against the far wall. She didn't even need to crawl over the wall, didn't need to touch her cold skin, or see the dried blood that all but obliterated her once pretty face, to know that Allison was dead.

But she did all those things.

Yes, she was dead, her body already cold to the touch. For a long, agonized moment Peggy knelt staring down at the lifeless form that had once been Allison. This was the reward for all her schemes, the result of her reckless machinations. There would be no fortune, no life of ease. She had gambled hugely—and she had lost.

But she would not die unavenged, Peggy vowed. She would find the authorities, she would tell them of this grisly wall and its secret. Those who had done this to Allison would pay.

"I swear it, darling," she whispered into the damp darkness, "I swear, they won't get away with this."

She wanted to take off her sweater and put it over

Allison's face, but she dared not, lest she alert them that someone had been here and discovered their secret. The last thing she wanted was to alarm them into flight before she had brought the authorities back. This time the sheriff would have to listen to her; this time she wasn't talking about a missing person, she was talking about cold-blooded, brutal murder.

She clambered back over the brick wall and started toward the steps.

And stopped. as she found herself face to face with Mrs. Marvel, waiting at the foot of the steps.

Chapter 25

"You," Mrs. Marvel said, her voice a hiss of hate. "I might have known—this is all your fault."

"You killed her," Peggy said. It was pointless to pretend—the woman had certainly seen her clambering over the half-completed wall.

"She was going to leave, to run out on me—me, the one who had thought up this entire scheme, who had made it all work. And she was going to take everything, have me thrown out."

Peggy's mind was darting frantically about, seeking some means of escape, while another part of her kept Mrs. Marvel occupied in talk.

"How did you get her to come back here?" she asked aloud. "She was already at my hotel, on her way up."

Mrs. Marvel laughed, a hoarse cackle that seemed to echo about the dusty, cobwebbed room. "That was easy. I played on her greed. I told her we had found a new will, changing everything. She was so frightened that she might lose the money after all, she came straight back with us without a whimper."

"Then why did you kill her?"

Mrs. Marvel came a step closer. The stairs behind her were open. If only, Peggy thought, she might get to the stairs, up them—she would have a chance to elude them in the dark, and reach her boat.

"Because she wouldn't listen to reason," Mrs. Marvel said, an edge of hysteria in her evil voice. "She refused to cooperate. She laughed at me, and tried to push past me. She was going to leave again. I picked up a vase, and struck her, and when she started to scream, I struck her again and again. . ."

Peggy tried to dart past her, but the woman was faster than she looked. She had just reached the bottom step when Mrs. Marvel grabbed her arm with such force that she nearly knocked Peggy off her feet. Peggy swayed and turned, trying to fight free of those amazingly powerful hands, hands that tried to reach her throat, tried to choke her. She slapped at them, and finally reached up, burying her fingers in that elegant gray hair.

To her further astonishment the hair came away, and the veiled hat with it, and Peggy was looking into the evil face of—Jack Lions.

He gave a shriek as the hair came loose. "Waldo. " he screamed. "Quick!"

He grabbed for his wig, as if keeping his identity concealed were the most important thing—and in that instant, Peggy broke free of his grasp. She stumbled backward, into a wine rack, and her clawing fingers closed over a bottle of wine. Jack, his wig askew, lumbered toward her. Peggy swung the bottle, catching him alongside the head, and he staggered away from her.

There was only one bare light bulb burning overhead. She swung the wine bottle at it. The glass broke, and the room was plunged into night. Whirling, she ran into the darkness, along the racks of wine.

"What's wrong?" It was Waldo's voice from the top of the stairs.

"That girl, her sister," Jack called back, "she's down here, she's found the body. Come on, we've got to find her."

"What's happened to the light?"

"Oh, never mind that, she can't get out of here—Come on!"

Peggy crouched breathlessly behind a row of bottles. Jack, Mrs. Denver, Mrs. Marvel—all one and the same. She thought back—their rooms, side by side, probably with a connecting door; the time she'd gone to see Mrs. Marvel and had had to wait, no doubt while he donned the wig and jumped into bed to conceal his masculine clothes. And the fact that they never appeared together; because they couldn't, of course; the veils and sunglasses, the odd feeling of repulsion she'd had whenever he tried to touch her; the womanish quality she'd noted in him, and at the same time, the masculine mannerisms of Mrs. Marvel.

It was all there, had been there all the time, if she'd only been clever enough to see. But she hadn't, and she had been thrown off by his obvious—or staged—desire for her—her foolish Leo vanity again, making a fool of her better judgment.

She heard Waldo's heavy tread on the steps—a whispered consultation. They would be searching for her, and somehow she must elude them and escape—but how? Jack had said she couldn't get out of here; were there no windows, no other doors?

She crept along an aisle, walking in a crouched position. Their voices had stopped. All about her the house was still again, listening, waiting, tensed for something to happen.

She bumped against a bottle. It rattled loudly in the stillness, setting her heart to pounding. She darted away, around another corner. It was like a cat and mouse game; where were they? For all she knew, she might be creeping directly toward them. And still she had found no windows, no doors. There *had* to be a way out of this basement.

She found one window at last, but it was tiny and high up in the wall—even if she could get to it she doubted that she would be able to squeeze through it. And they would certainly hear her trying, and get to her before she could escape through it.

She had circled her way around almost to the stairs again. She listened, and still there was no sound of the two men. She flattened herself against a rack and peered cautiously around the corner.

There was no one there. The path to the steps lay open before her. If only she could reach them, get up them, she would be all right. She reached down and slipped her shoes off. Her hands were trembling and her legs felt as if they would melt beneath her. She wondered that they did not hear the pounding of her heart.

This is it, she thought, and taking a deep breath she dashed from her hiding place toward the stairs. She reached them, grabbing the railing and fairly flinging herself upward—only to realize too late that the way was blocked above by the heavy figure of Mrs. Brunner.

"Stop her," Mrs. Marvel's voice cried from behind.

For a second or two Peggy stood frozen in indecision, and then it was too late. Even as she started to race up the stairs, hoping perhaps she could get past the housekeeper, she felt Waldo's powerful arm encircling her, and she knew escape was impossible.

She was dragged kicking and struggling back down to the foot of the stairs, and there once again she found herself face to face with Mrs. Marvel—or Jack, as she now was forced to think of him, for with the wig at its Humpty Dumpty it could not be put back together again.

"And now," Jack said, his voice thick with menace, "we shall have to deal with you, my lovely."

Chapter 26

"What'll we do with her?" Waldo asked.

"Do?" Jack chuckled. "Why, there's only one thing to do. She came back here because she wanted to be with her sister, didn't she?"

Peggy felt a chill of horror sweep over her. All the old stories—Edgar Allan Poe's tales—to be buried alive, in this musty cellar.

"You can't," she cried, trying again to struggle free, but she was no match for Waldo's brute strength.

"But it's what you wanted, isn't it?" Jack said, laughing. "I said that girl won't be satisfied until she gets the same as her sister, but he wouldn't listen. Oh, no, she's too pretty, he said, we can't harm her. The ninny, if he'd listened to me we'd have gotten rid of you long ago, that was what I wanted. And I very nearly succeeded too, the night I sent Waldo to your hotel room. I thought then we'd be finished with you."

"You—you're mad," Peggy gasped.

"Don't say that!" It was a shriek, a furious denial. He waved his hand toward the brickwork nearby. "Put her in there. Tie her up, or better yet, knock her out. By the time she wakes up, she'll be sealed away in her tomb, with her blasted sister. And we'll be rid of both of them forever.''

Peggy screamed, her cry echoing wildly about the room, but even as she screamed she knew there was no one to hear. Waldo clamped a hand over her mouth, and unable to stop him, she stared in horror as he half dragged her, half carried her to the brick wall. She felt herself being lifted bodily over the wall and into the recess next to poor Allison's dead body. The room seemed to spin as consciousness threatened to leave her. She fought to retain her senses—the horror of waking up to find herself buried alive was almost more than she could bear.

It was useless. In a moment Waldo was tying her hands together into a corner, knocking the breath from her. She lay in a daze and saw, in the dim light, mortar being spread on a brick, and another brick being placed atop it. Then another, and another—it was happening. They were actually sealing her in here with Allison's body, with no chance of escape.

She screamed again, hysterically this time, and scrambled to her feet, staggering to the brickwork. She tried to push the bricks away, but Waldo gave her a brutal shove, slamming her back against the wall.

She thought she would go mad from the horror—she thought she *had* lost her mind, because even as she stared at the bricks going into place, she saw the wall behind Waldo suddenly swing open—and there, to her amazement, was Alex, with a gun in his hand.

Waldo saw him too, and he tried to hit him with the brick in his hand. But Alex ducked the blow and instead brought the butt of his gun down across the back of

Waldo's head. The huge man sagged and fell to the floor in a heap.

Mrs. Brunner gave a cry and rushed to her husband's prone form. Jack, after a wild-eyed moment, tried to run to the steps, but Alex caught him by a trailing piece of chiffon and jerked him back around.

"Not so fast," he said, shoving Jack back against a wall. "When I get Peggy out of th re, I may send you in to take her place."

For a moment Jack fought against him, kicking and clawing like a woman. But he was not fighting Peggy now, he was fighting a man who was used to hard work, who had built his muscles working in vineyards and wineries, and soon he saw that the struggle was futile. He stopped fighting and collapsed into a wailing, trembling travesty of a heartbroken woman.

"Oh, it's all gone wrong," he sobbed. "The stars lied to me, they said I couldn't fail. And they lied, they lied."

"Maybe you just read them wrong," Alex said, stepping across the brick wall to lift Peggy out. "Mine said I was going to find the love of my life."

He untied her wrists and she clung weakly to him, still hardly able to believe that she was not sealed for eternity behind that wall of bricks. All the while Jack stood huddled against the wall, crying loudly, and moaning over and over, "They lied, the stars lied."

The morning light glinted on the water. They stood at the little dock watching the launch in which the lake patrol was taking away the prisoners. Jack still wore the lavender chiffon dress he had worn the night before, but in the confusion he had finally lost his wig and hat

217

altogether. He made a grotesque appearance, makeup smeared, earrings dangling, and his short, masculine haircut unwigged. He had lost all his spirit, and sat staring morosely into the distance, at what private vision they could not say.

"You never did say how you happened to come back a day early?" Peggy said, leaning happily into Alex's embrace.

"Partly an odd hunch—or call it ESP. Something seemed to be drawing me back. And on top of that, I'd forgotten some papers of my father's that I needed for the attorneys. So I came back for them. I had already gone up to his room when I heard you scream, and the shortest way down to the basement was that secret passageway, the one Melissa had mentioned."

"How do you suppose she knew about that?" Peggy asked, looking up into his handsome face.

"We'll never know. Maybe Father told her about it himself."

"Or maybe she really did remember it from her childhood," Peggy said.

"Maybe. I know one thing, she really wanted to be Melissa, and Father wanted the same thing. And as far as the official reports will show, she was."

"She'd like it that way." Peggy looked out onto the lake; the launch was nearly out of sight. "Poor Jack," she said with a sigh.

"A real split personality," Alex said. "I think in his mind he really was two different people. Maybe at first it was a deliberate disguise. He was here in the house, but he was insignificant, no one ever paid any attention to him anymore. But he knew Father was into astrology, and he knew the old man pined for his lost

Melissa; and Jack must have somehow introduced 'Mrs. Marvel' into the house, and into Father's confidence. But I think over the years, he came to think of her as another person. I think he really did hate her, because she had come to dominate, she was so much stronger than he was.''

''But he still had the other side to his personality,'' she said, turning with him back toward the house. ''I think that when he was Jack, he really was attracted to me.''

''Leo vanity, that's all,'' he said teasingly, squeezing her waist.

''Oh no.'' She pulled free of him and stared at him, shaking her head.

''What's wrong?'' He looked puzzled.

''That's how all this started,'' she said, ''with astrology, and Leo, and lions.''

He laughed and pulled her back to him. ''And that's how it will end, too. After all, you're going to be a Lion too. Mrs. Alex Lions.''

They kissed. They were near the gate, and when at last the kiss ended, she found herself looking past his shoulder at one of the great stone beasts overhead. But now the animal no longer looked threatening, he looked benign, and protective—like the Leo of her sign.